THE
DARK
SIDE

THE
DARK
SIDE

Edited by Damon Knight

1965

Doubleday & Company, Inc.
Garden City, New York

Acknowledgments

"The Black Ferris," by Ray Bradbury, copyright 1948 by Weird Tales; reprinted by permission of the author

"They," by Robert A. Heinlein, copyright 1941 by Street & Smith Publications, Inc.; reprinted by permission of the author

"Mistake Inside," by James Blish, copyright 1948 by Better Publications, Inc.; reprinted by permission of the author

"Trouble with Water," by H. L. Gold, copyright 1939 by Street & Smith Publications, Inc.; reprinted by permission of the author

"C/o Mr. Makepeace," by Peter Phillips, copyright 1954 by Fantasy House, Inc.; reprinted by permission of Scott Meredith Literary Agency, Inc.

"The Golem," by Avram Davidson, copyright © 1955 by Fantasy House, Inc.; reprinted by permission of the author

"The Story of the Late Mr. Elvesham" by H. G. Wells from *Complete Short Stories of H. G. Wells;* reprinted by permission of the Executors of H. G. Wells

"It," by Theodore Sturgeon, copyright 1940 by Street & Smith Publications, Inc.; reprinted by permission of the author

"Nellthu," by Anthony Boucher, copyright © 1955 by Anthony Boucher; reprinted by permission of Willis Kingsley Wing

"Casey Agonistes," by Richard McKenna, copyright © 1958 by Mercury Press, Inc.; reprinted by permission of the author

"Eye for Iniquity," by T. L. Sherred, copyright 1953 by Galaxy Publishing Corp.; reprinted by permission of the author

"The Man Who Never Grew Young," by Fritz Leiber, copyright 1947 by Fritz Leiber, Jr.; reprinted by permission of August Derleth

for TED and GINNY

CONTENTS

CONTENTS

INTRODUCTION

"Fantasy" is a word that makes many people wince and turn away; if you are one of these, I would like to say at the outset that I sympathize with you. The word is a catchall for everything in fiction from *Peter Rabbit* to *The Tempest,* including much that is slovenly, formless, trite, and foolish. But it is also the generally accepted term for the kind of rigorous, ingeniously contrived story of imagination that I want to talk about here.

Think of imaginative fiction as a sphere, a planet like Mercury, sunlit on one side and dark on the other. We draw a line around the middle and call the bright side science fiction, the dark side fantasy: but it is really all one thing. Not by coincidence, almost every major writer of what we call "science fiction" has also written what we call "fantasy," and has written it brilliantly. Indeed, except for their themes, the stories in this book are much more like science fiction than like traditional fantasy. They are written in modern prose and they take place, by and large, in modern settings. More to the point, they follow the prime rule of science fiction: the author is allowed only one fantastic assumption; thereafter his story must be developed logically, consistently, and without violating known fact.

These categories, like all others, have their limitations. Much of science fiction is pretty grim, and much fantasy, like "Trouble with Water" and "Eye for Iniquity," is anything but. Yet the dark side exists. Every human being is like an eye in a sphere that is half darkness, half light; and the eye always turns to face the brightness of the world of sensation, the world of order, logic, and common sense. That is the side you are facing now, as you read these words in the bright little disk of your visual field. But you have only to stop for a moment to be aware of the dark half sphere behind you—the darkness of wonder and terror, of forgotten things, impossible things, things that have no names and no faces. Consciousness is an act of exclusion; to be aware of one thing, you must turn away from hundreds of others that go on swimming nevertheless, gray and formless, in the darkness of your mind.

The oldest story in this book is "The Story of the Late Mr. Elvesham," by H. G. Wells (1896); but in a sense, the closest to traditional fantasy is Ray Bradbury's "The Black Ferris," published in *Weird Tales* in 1948, which eventually grew into Bradbury's novel *Something Wicked This Way Comes*.

Weird Tales was an odd little pulp magazine, devoted to stories of the supernatural. It was founded in 1923 and lasted thirty-one years. We should be glad it did, if only because it provided a seed-bed for the growth of Ray Bradbury's remarkable talent.

Bradbury took what he wanted from the stock furniture of the supernatural horror story, and transformed it into something uniquely his own. This is a story about time, one of the standard themes of science fiction, and there is even a time machine in it, of a sort; but it is fantasy, not s.f.—not because the author makes no attempt to explain how his machine works (neither did Wells, in *The Time Machine*), but because of the black wind that sighs through the story from the beginning, "like a dark bat flying over the cold lake, bones rattling in the night. . . ."

Ray Bradbury

THE BLACK FERRIS

The carnival had come to town like an October wind, like a dark bat flying over the cold lake, bones rattling in the night, mourning, sighing, whispering up the tents in the dark rain. It stayed on for a month by the gray, restless lake of October, in the black weather and increasing storms and leaden skies.

During the third week, at twilight on a Thursday, the two small boys walked along the lake shore in the cold wind.

"Aw, I don't believe you," said Peter.

"Come on, and I'll show you," said Hank.

They left wads of spit behind them all along the moist brown sand of the crashing shore. They ran to the lonely carnival grounds. It had been raining. The carnival lay by the sounding lake with nobody buying tickets from the flaky black booths, nobody hoping to get the salted hams from the whining roulette wheels, and none of the thin-fat freaks on the big platforms. The midway was silent, all the gray tents hissing on the wind like gigantic prehistoric wings. At eight o'clock perhaps, ghastly lights would flash on, voices would shout, music would go out over the lake. Now there was only a blind hunchback sitting on a black booth, feeling of the cracked china cup from which he was drinking some perfumed brew.

"There," said Hank, pointing.

The black Ferris wheel rose like an immense light-bulbed constellation against the cloudy sky, silent.

"I still don't believe what you said about it," said Peter.

"You wait, I saw it happen. I don't know how, but it did. You know how carnivals are; all funny. Okay; this one's even *funnier*."

Peter let himself be led to the high green hiding place of a tree.

Suddenly, Hank stiffened. *"Hist!* There's Mr. Cooger, the carnival man, now!" Hidden, they watched.

Mr. Cooger, a man of some thirty-five years, dressed in sharp bright clothes, a lapel carnation, hair greased with oil, drifted under the tree, a brown derby hat on his head. He had arrived in town three weeks before, shaking his brown derby hat at people on the street from inside his shiny red Ford, tooting the horn.

Now Mr. Cooger nodded at the little blind hunchback, spoke a word. The hunchback blindly, fumbling, locked Mr. Cooger into a black seat and sent him whirling up into the ominous twilight sky. Machinery hummed.

"See!" whispered Hank. "The Ferris wheel's going the wrong way. Backwards instead of forwards!"

"So what?" said Peter.

"Watch!"

The black Ferris wheel whirled twenty-five times around. Then the blind hunchback put out his pale hands and halted the machinery. The Ferris wheel stopped, gently swaying, at a certain black seat.

A ten-year-old boy stepped out. He walked off across the whispering carnival ground, in the shadows.

Peter almost fell from his limb. He searched the Ferris wheel with his eyes. "Where's Mr. Cooger!"

Hank poked him. "You wouldn't believe! Now *see!*"

"Where's Mr. Cooger at!"

"Come on, quick, run!" Hank dropped and was sprinting before he hit the ground.

Under giant chestnut trees, next to the ravine, the lights were burning in Mrs. Foley's white mansion. Piano music tinkled. Within the warm windows, people moved. Outside, it began to rain, despondently, irrevocably, forever and ever.

"I'm *so* wet," grieved Peter, crouching in the bushes. "Like someone squirted me with a hose. How much longer do we wait?"

"Sh!" said Hank, cloaked in wet mystery.

They had followed the little boy from the Ferris wheel up through town, down dark streets to Mrs. Foley's ravine house. Now, inside the warm dining room of the house the strange little boy sat at dinner, forking and spooning rich lamb chops and mashed potatoes.

"I know his name," whispered Hank, quickly. "My Mom told me about him the other day. She said, 'Hank, you hear about the li'l orphan boy moved in Mrs. Foley's? Well, his name is Joseph Pikes and he just came to Mrs. Foley's one day about two weeks ago and said how he was an orphan run away and could he have something to eat, and him and Mrs. Foley been getting on like hot apple pie ever since.' That's what my Mom said," finished Hank, peering through the steamy Foley window. Water dripped from his nose. He held onto Peter who was twitching with cold. "Pete, I didn't like his looks from the first, I didn't. He looked—mean."

"I'm scared," said Peter, frankly wailing. "I'm cold and hungry and I don't know what this's all about."

"Gosh, you're dumb!" Hank shook his head, eyes shut in disgust. "Don't you see, three weeks ago the carnival came. And about the same time this little ole orphan shows up at Mrs. Foley's. And Mrs. Foley's son died a long time ago one night one winter, and she's never been the same, so here's this little ole orphan boy who butters her all around."

"Oh," said Peter, shaking.

"Come on," said Hank. They marched to the front door and banged the lion knocker.

After awhile the door opened and Mrs. Foley looked out.

"You're all wet, come in," she said. "My land," she herded them into the hall. "What do you want?" she said, bending over them, a tall lady with lace on her full bosom and a pale thin face with white hair over it. "You're Henry Walterson, aren't you?"

Hank nodded, glancing fearfully at the dining room where the strange little boy looked up from his eating. "Can we see you alone, ma'm?" And when the old lady looked palely surprised, Hank crept over and shut the hall door and whispered at her. "We got to warn you about something, it's about that boy come to live with you, that orphan?"

The hall grew suddenly cold. Mrs. Foley drew herself high and stiff. "Well?"

"He's from the carnival, and he ain't a boy, he's a man, and he's planning on living here with you until he finds where your money is and then run off with it some night, and people will look for him but because they'll be looking for a little ten-year-old boy they won't recognize him when he walks by a thirty-five year man, named Mr. Cooger!" cried Hank.

"What *are* you talking about?" declared Mrs. Foley.

"The carnival and the Ferris wheel and this strange man, Mr. Cooger, the Ferris wheel going backward and making him younger, I don't know how, and him coming here as a boy, and you can't trust him, because when he has your money he'll get on the Ferris wheel and it'll go *forward,* and he'll be thirty-five years old again, and the boy'll be gone forever!"

"Goodnight, Henry Walterson, don't *ever* come back!" shouted Mrs. Foley.

The door slammed. Peter and Hank found themselves in the rain once more. It soaked into and into them, cold and complete.

"Smart guy," snorted Peter. "Now you fixed it. Suppose he heard us, suppose he comes and *kills* us in our beds tonight, to shut us all up for keeps!"

"He wouldn't do that," said Hank.

"Wouldn't he?" Peter seized Hank's arm. "Look."

In the big bay window of the dining room now the mesh curtain pulled aside. Standing there in the pink light, his hand made into a menacing fist, was the little orphan boy. His face was horrible to see, the teeth bared, the eyes hateful, the lips mouthing out terrible words. That was all. The orphan boy was there only a second, then gone. The curtain fell into place. The rain poured down upon the house. Hank and Peter walked slowly home in the storm.

During supper, Father looked at Hank and said, "If you don't catch pneumonia, I'll be surprised. Soaked, you were, by God! What's this about the carnival?"

Hank fussed at his mashed potatoes, occasionally looking

at the rattling windows. "You know Mr. Cooger, the carnival man, Dad?"

"The one with the pink carnation in his lapel?" asked Father.

"Yes!" Hank sat up. "You've seen him around?"

"He stays down the street at Mrs. O'Leary's boarding house, got a room in back. Why?"

"Nothing," said Hank, his face glowing.

After supper Hank put through a call to Peter on the phone. At the other end of the line, Peter sounded miserable with coughing.

"Listen, Pete!" said Hank. "I see it all now. When that li'l ole orphan boy, Joseph Pikes, gets Mrs. Foley's money, he's got a good plan."

"What?"

"He'll stick around town as the carnival man, living in a room at Mrs. O'Leary's. That way nobody'll get suspicious of him. Everybody'll be looking for that nasty little boy and he'll be gone. And he'll be walking around, all disguised as the carnival man. That way, nobody'll suspect the carnival at all. It would look funny if the carnival suddenly pulled up stakes."

"Oh," said Peter, sniffling.

"So we got to act fast," said Hank.

"Nobody'll believe us, I tried to tell my folks but they said hogwash!" moaned Peter.

"We got to act tonight, anyway. Because why? Because he's gonna try to kill us! We're the only ones that know and if we tell the police to keep an eye on him, he's the one who stole Mrs. Foley's money in cahoots with the orphan boy, he won't live peaceful. I bet he just tries something tonight. So, I tell you, meet me at Mrs. Foley's in half an hour."

"Aw," said Peter.

"You wanna die?"

"No." Thoughtfully.

"Well, then. Meet me there and I bet we see that orphan boy sneaking out with the money, tonight, and running back down to the carnival grounds with it, when Mrs. Foley's asleep. I'll see you there. So long, Pete!"

"Young man," said Father, standing behind him as he hung up the phone. "You're not going anywhere. You're going straight up to bed. Here." He marched Hank upstairs. "Now hand me out everything you got on." Hank undressed. "There're no other clothes in your room are there?" asked Father. "No, sir, they're all in the hall closet," said Hank, disconsolately.

"Good," said Dad and shut and locked the door.

Hank stood there, naked. "Holy Cow," he said.

"Go to bed," said Father.

Peter arrived at Mrs. Foley's house at about nine-thirty, sneezing, lost in a vast raincoat and mariner's cap. He stood like a small water hydrant on the street, mourning softly over his fate. The lights in the Foley house were warmly on upstairs. Peter waited for a half an hour, looking at the rain-drenched slick streets of night.

Finally there was a darting paleness, a rustle in wet bushes.

"Hank?" Peter questioned the bushes.

"Yeah." Hank stepped out.

"Gosh," said Peter, staring. "You're—you're *naked!*"

"I ran all the way," said Hank. "Dad wouldn't let me out."

"You'll get pneumonia," said Peter.

The lights in the house went out.

"Duck," cried Hank, bounding behind some bushes. They waited. "Pete," said Hank. "You're wearing pants, aren't you?"

"Sure," said Pete.

"Well, you're wearing a raincoat, and nobody'll know, so lend me your pants," asked Hank.

A reluctant transaction was made. Hank pulled the pants on.

The rain let up. The clouds began to break apart.

In about ten minutes a small figure emerged from the house, bearing a large paper sack filled with some enormous loot or other.

"There he is," whispered Hank.

"There he goes!" cried Peter.

The orphan boy ran swiftly.

"Get after him!" cried Hank.

They gave chase through the chestnut trees, but the orphan boy was swift, up the hill, through the night streets of town, down past the rail yards, past the factories, to the midway of the deserted carnival. Hank and Peter were poor seconds, Peter weighted as he was with the heavy raincoat, and Hank frozen with cold. The thumping of Hank's bare feet sounded through the town.

"Hurry, Pete! We can't let him get to that Ferris wheel before we do, if he changes back into a man we'll never prove anything!"

"I'm hurrying!" But Pete was left behind as Hank thudded on alone in the clearing weather.

"Yah!" mocked the orphan boy, darting away, no more than a shadow ahead, now. Now vanishing into the carnival yard.

Hank stopped at the edge of the carnival lot. The Ferris wheel was going up and up into the sky, a big nebula of stars caught on the dark earth and turning forward and forward, instead of backward, and there sat Joseph Pikes in a green painted bucket-seat, laughing up and around and down and up and around and down at little old Hank standing there, and the little blind hunchback had his hand on the roaring, oily black machine that made the Ferris wheel go ahead and ahead. The midway was deserted because of the rain. The merry-go-round was still, but its music played and crashed in the open spaces. And Joseph Pikes rode up into the cloudy sky and came down and each time he went around he was a year older, his laughing changed, grew deep, his face changed, the bones of it, the mean eyes of it, the wild hair of it, sitting there in the green bucket-seat whirling, whirling swiftly, laughing into the bleak heavens where now and again a last split of lightning showed itself.

Hank ran forward at the hunchback by the machine. On the way he picked up a tent spike. "Here now!" yelled the hunchback. The black Ferris wheel whirled around. "You!" stormed the hunchback, fumbling out. Hank hit him in the kneecap and danced away. "Ouch!" screamed the man, falling forward. He tried to reach the machine brake to stop the Ferris wheel. When he put his hand on the brake, Hank ran in and slammed the tent spike against the fingers, mashing them. He hit them twice. The man held his hand in his other hand, howling. He kicked at Hank. Hank grabbed the foot, pulled, the man slipped in the mud and fell. Hank hit him on the head, shouting.

The Ferris wheel went around and around and around.

"Stop, stop the wheel!" cried Joseph Pikes-Mr. Cooger flung up in a stormy cold sky in the bubbled constellation of whirl and rush and wind.

"I can't move," groaned the hunchback. Hank jumped on his chest and they thrashed, biting, kicking.

"Stop, stop the wheel!" cried Mr. Cooger, a man, a different man and voice this time, coming around in panic, going up into the roaring hissing sky of the Ferris wheel. The wind blew through the high dark wheel spokes. "Stop, stop, oh, please stop the wheel!"

Hank leaped up from the sprawled hunchback. He started in on the brake mechanism, hitting it, jamming it, putting chunks of metal in it, tying it with rope, now and again hitting at the crawling weeping dwarf.

"Stop, stop, stop the wheel!" wailed a voice high in the night where the windy moon was coming out of the vaporous white clouds now. "Stop . . ." The voice faded.

Now the carnival was ablaze with sudden light. Men sprang out of tents, came running. Hank felt himself jerked into the air with oaths and beatings rained on him. From a distance there was a sound of Peter's voice and behind Peter, at full tilt, a police officer with pistol drawn.

"Stop, stop the wheel!" In the wind the voice sighed away. The voice repeated and repeated.

The dark carnival men tried to apply the brake. Nothing happened. The machine hummed and turned the wheel around and around. The mechanism was jammed.

"Stop!" cried the voice one last time.

Silence.

Without a word the Ferris wheel flew in a circle, a high system of electric stars and metal and seats. There was no sound now but the sound of the motor which died and stopped. The Ferris wheel coasted for a minute, all the carnival people looking up at it, the policeman looking up at it, Hank and Peter looking up at it.

The Ferris wheel stopped. A crowd had gathered at the noise. A few fishermen from the wharfhouse, a few switchmen from the rail yards. The Ferris wheel stood whining and stretching in the wind.

"Look," everybody said.

The policeman turned and the carnival people turned and the fishermen turned and they all looked at the occupant in the black-painted seat at the bottom of the ride. The wind touched and moved the black wooden seat in a gentle rocking rhythm, crooning over the occupant in the dim carnival light.

A skeleton sat there, a paper bag of money in its hands, a brown derby hat on its head.

Many of the writers in this book, like Ray Bradbury, have pulp-magazine backgrounds, and you will find bits and pieces of pulp writing in their stories, woven in just because it was the handiest material, like the rags and string in a bird's nest. But here is a story which owes nothing to conventional popular fiction and is really unclassifiable. We toss it into the "fantasy" bin because it does not fit anywhere else; its basic assumption is one we must believe to be false. (Solipsism, as Kate Wilhelm has pointed out, is the one philosophical belief to which nobody can ever convert anyone else.) Yet it is as closely reasoned, as faithful to observed reality—and as irrefutable—as the hardest of hard s.f.

This brilliant and compact story has the hallmark of great fiction: you will never be quite the same again after you have read it.

Robert A. Heinlein

THEY

They would not let him alone.

They never would let him alone. He realized that that was part of the plot against him—never to leave him in peace, never to give him a chance to mull over the lies they had told him, time enough to pick out the flaws, and to figure out the truth for himself.

That damned attendant this morning! He had come busting in with his breakfast tray, waking him, and causing him to forget his dream. If only he could remember that dream—

Someone was unlocking the door. He ignored it.

"Howdy, old boy. They tell me you refused your breakfast?" Dr. Hayward's professionally kindly mask hung over his bed.

"I wasn't hungry."

"But we can't have that. You'll get weak, and then I won't be able to get you well completely. Now get up and get your clothes on and I'll order an eggnog for you. Come on, that's a good fellow!"

Unwilling, but still less willing at that moment to enter into any conflict of wills, he got out of bed and slipped on his bathrobe. "That's better," Hayward approved. "Have a cigarette?"

"No, thank you."

The doctor shook his head in a puzzled fashion. "Darned

if I can figure you out. Loss of interest in physical pleasures does not fit your type of case."

"What is my type of case?" he inquired in flat tones.

"Tut! Tut!" Hayward tried to appear roguish. "If medicos told their professional secrets, they might have to work for a living."

"What is my type of case?"

"Well—the label doesn't matter, does it? Suppose *you* tell me. I really know nothing about your case as yet. Don't you think it is about time you talked?"

"I'll play chess with you."

"All right, all right." Hayward made a gesture of impatient concession. "We've played chess every day for a week. If you will talk, I'll play chess."

What could it matter? If he was right, they already understood perfectly that he had discovered their plot; there was nothing to be gained by concealing the obvious. Let them try to argue him out of it. Let the tail go with the hide! To hell with it!

He got out the chessmen and commenced setting them up. "What do you know of my case so far?"

"Very little. Physical examination, negative. Past history, negative. High intelligence, as shown by your record in school and your success in your profession. Occasional fits of moodiness, but nothing exceptional. The only positive information was the incident that caused you to come here for treatment."

"To be brought here, you mean. Why should it cause comment?"

"Well, good gracious, man—if you barricade yourself in

your room and insist that your wife is plotting against you, don't you expect people to notice?"

"But she *was* plotting against me—and so are you. White, or black?"

"Black—it's your turn to attack. Why do you think we are 'plotting against you'?"

"It's an involved story, and goes way back into my early childhood. There was an immediate incident, however—" He opened by advancing the white king's knight to KB3. Hayward's eyebrows raised.

"You make a piano attack?"

"Why not? You know that it is not safe for me to risk a gambit with you."

The doctor shrugged his shoulders and answered the opening. "Suppose we start with your early childhood. It may shed more light than more recent incidents. Did you feel that you were persecuted as a child?"

"No!" He half rose from his chair. "When I was a child I was sure of myself. I knew then. I tell you; I knew! Life was worth while, and I knew it. I was at peace with myself and my surroundings. Life was good and I was good, and I assumed that the creatures around me were like myself."

"And weren't they?"

"Not at all! Particularly the children. I didn't know what viciousness was until I was turned loose with other 'children.' The little devils! And I was expected to be like them and play with them."

The doctor nodded. "I know. The herd compulsion. Children can be pretty savage at times."

"You've missed the point. This wasn't any healthy roughness; these creatures were *different*—not like myself at all.

They *looked* like me, but they were *not* like me. If I tried to say anything to one of them about anything that mattered to me, all I could get was a stare and a scornful laugh. Then they would find some way to punish me for having said it."

Hayward nodded. "I see what you mean. How about grownups?"

"That is something different. Adults don't matter to children at first—or rather, they did not matter to me. They were too big, and they did not bother me, and they were busy with things that did not enter into my considerations. It was only when I noticed that my presence affected them that I began to wonder about them."

"How do you mean?"

"Well, they never did the things when I was around that they did when I was not around."

Hayward looked at him carefully. "Won't that statement take quite a lot of justifying? How do you know what they did when you weren't around?"

He acknowledged the point. "But I used to catch them just stopping. If I came into a room, the conversation would stop suddenly, and then it would pick up about the weather or something equally inane. Then I took to hiding and listening and looking. Adults did not behave the same way in my presence as out of it."

"Your move, I believe. But see here, old man—that was when you were a child. Every child passes through that phase. Now that you are a man, you must see the adult point of view. Children are strange creatures and have to be protected—at least, we do protect them—from many adult interests. There is a whole code of conventions in the matter that—"

"Yes, yes," he interrupted impatiently, "I know all that. Nevertheless, I noticed enough and remembered enough that was never clear to me later. And it put me on my guard to notice the next thing."

"Which was?" He noticed that the doctor's eyes were averted as he adjusted a castle's position.

"The things I saw people doing and heard them talking about were never of any importance. They *must* be doing something else."

"I don't follow you."

"You don't choose to follow me. I'm telling this to you in exchange for a game of chess."

"Why do you like to play chess so well?"

"Because it is the only thing in the world where I can see all the factors and understand all the rules. Never mind—I saw all around me this enormous plant, cities, farms, factories, churches, schools, homes, railroads, luggage, roller coasters, trees, saxophones, libraries, people and animals. People that looked like me and who should have felt very much like me, if what I was told was the truth. But what did they appear to be doing? 'They went to work to earn the money to buy the food to get the strength to go to work to get the strength to buy the food to earn the money to go to—' until they fell over dead. Any slight variation in the basic pattern did not matter, for they always fell over dead. And everybody tried to tell me that I should be doing the same thing. I knew better!"

The doctor gave him a look apparently intended to denote helpless surrender and laughed. "I can't argue with you. Life does look like that, and maybe it is just that futile. But it is the only life we have. Why not make up your mind to enjoy it as much as possible?"

"Oh, no!" He looked both sulky and stubborn. "You can't peddle nonsense to me by claiming to be fresh out of sense. How do I know? Because all this complex stage setting, all these swarms of actors, could not have been put here just to make idiot noises at each other. Some other explanation but not that one. An insanity as enormous, as complex, as the one around me had to be planned. I've found the plan!"

"Which is?"

He noticed that the doctor's eyes were again averted.

"It is a play intended to divert me, to occupy my mind and confuse me, to keep me so busy with details that I will not have time to think about the meaning. You are all in it, every one of you." He shook his finger in the doctor's face. "Most of them may be helpless automatons, but you're not. You are one of the conspirators. You've been sent in as a troubleshooter to try to force me to go back to playing the role assigned to me!"

He saw that the doctor was waiting for him to quiet down.

"Take it easy," Hayward finally managed to say. "Maybe it is all a conspiracy, but why do you think that you have been singled out for special attention? Maybe it is a joke on all of us. Why couldn't I be one of the victims as well as yourself?"

"Got you!" He pointed a long finger at Hayward. "That is the essence of the plot. All of these creatures have been set up to look like me in order to prevent me from realizing that I was the center of the arrangements. But I have noticed the key fact, the mathematically inescapable fact, that I am unique. Here am I, sitting on the inside. The world extends outward from me. I am the center—"

"Easy, man, easy! Don't you realize that the world looks that way to me, too? We are each the center of the universe—"

"Not so! That is what you have tried to make me believe, that I am just one of millions more just like me. Wrong! If they were like me, then I could get into communication with them. I can't. I have tried and tried and I can't. I've sent out my inner thoughts, seeking some one other being who has them, too. What have I gotten back? Wrong answers, jarring incongruities, meaningless obscenity. I've tried, I tell you. God!—how I've tried! But there is nothing out there to speak to me—nothing but emptiness and otherness!"

"Wait a minute. Do you mean to say that you think there is nobody home at my end of the line? Don't you believe that I am alive and conscious?"

He regarded the doctor soberly. "Yes, I think you are probably alive, but you are one of the others—my antagonists. But you have set thousands of others around me whose faces are blank, not *lived in,* and whose speech is a meaningless reflex of noise."

"Well, then, if you concede that I am an ego, why do you insist that I am so very different from yourself?"

"Why? Wait!" He pushed back from the chess table and strode over to the wardrobe, from which he took out a violin case.

While he was playing, the lines of suffering smoothed out of his face and his expression took on a relaxed beatitude. For a while he recaptured the emotions, but not the knowledge, which he had possessed in dreams. The melody proceeded easily from proposition to proposition with inescapable, unforced logic. He finished with a triumphant statement of the essential thesis and turned to the doctor. "Well?"

"Hm-m-m." He seemed to detect an even greater degree of caution in the doctor's manner. "It's an odd bit, but remarkable. 'S pity you didn't take up the violin seriously. You could have made quite a reputation. You could even now. Why don't you do it? You could afford to, I believe."

He stood and stared at the doctor for a long moment, then shook his head as if trying to clear it. "It's no use," he said slowly, "no use at all. There is no possibility of communication. I am alone." He replaced the instrument in its case and returned to the chess table. "My move, I believe?"

"Yes. Guard your queen."

He studied the board. "Not necessary. I no longer need my queen. Check."

The doctor interposed a pawn to parry the attack.

He nodded. "You use your pawns well, but I have learned to anticipate your play. Check again—and mate, I think."

The doctor examined the new situation. "No," he decided, "no—not quite." He retreated from the square under attack. "Not checkmate—stalemate at the worst. Yes, another stalemate."

He was upset by the doctor's visit. He *couldn't* be wrong, basically, yet the doctor had certainly pointed out logical holes in his position. From a logical standpoint the whole world might be a fraud perpetrated on everybody. But logic means nothing—logic itself was a fraud, starting with unproved assumptions and capable of proving anything. The world is what it is!—and carries its own evidence of trickery.

But does it? What did he have to go on? Could he lay down a line between known facts and everything else and then make a reasonable interpretation of the world, based on facts alone—an interpretation free from complexities of logic and no hidden assumptions of points not certain? Very well—

First fact, himself. He knew himself directly. He existed.

Second facts, the evidence of his "five senses," everything that he himself saw and heard and smelled and tasted with his physical senses. Subject to their limitations, he must believe his senses. Without them he was entirely solitary, shut up in a locker of bone, blind, deaf, cut off, the only being in the world.

And that was not the case. He knew that he did not invent the information brought to him by his senses. There had to be something else out there. Some *otherness* that produced the things his senses recorded. All philosophies that claimed that the physical world around him did not exist except in his imagination were sheer nonsense.

But beyond that, what? Were there any third facts on which he could rely? No, not at this point. He could not afford to believe anything that he was told, or that he read, or that was implicitly assumed to be true about the world around him. No, he could not believe any of it, for the sum total of what he had been told and read and been taught in school was contradictory, so senseless, so wildly insane that none of it could be believed unless he personally confirmed it.

Wait a minute— The very telling of these lies, these senseless contradictions, was a fact in itself, known to him directly. To that extent they were data, probably very important data.

The world as it had been shown to him was a piece of unreason, an idiot's dream. Yet it was on too mammoth a scale to be without some reason. He came wearily back to his original point: Since the world could not be as crazy as it appeared to be, it must necessarily have been arranged to appear crazy in order to deceive him as to the truth.

Why had they done it to him? And what was the truth behind the sham? There must be some clue in the deception itself. What thread ran through it all? Well, in the first place he had been given a superabundance of explanations of the world around him, philosophies, religions, "common sense" explanations. Most of them were so clumsy, so obviously inadequate, or meaningless, that they could hardly have expected him to take them seriously. They must have intended them simply as misdirection.

But there were certain basic assumptions running through all the hundreds of explanations of the craziness around him. It must be these basic assumptions that he was expected to believe. For example, there was the deep-seated assumption that he was a "human being," essentially like millions of others around him and billions more in the past and the future.

That was nonsense! He had never once managed to get into real communication with all those *things* that looked so much like him but were so different. In the agony of his loneliness, he had deceived himself that Alice understood him and was a being like him. He knew now that he had suppressed and refused to examine thousands of little discrepancies because he could not bear the thought of returning to complete loneliness. He had needed to believe that his wife was a living, breathing being of his own kind who understood his inner thoughts. He had refused to consider the possibility that she was simply a mirror, an echo —or something unthinkably worse.

He had found a mate, and the world was tolerable, even though dull, stupid, and full of petty annoyance. He was moderately happy and had put away his suspicions. He had accepted, quite docilely, the treadmill he was expected to use, until a slight mischance had momentarily cut through the fraud—then his suspicions had returned with impounded force; the bitter knowledge of his childhood had been confirmed.

He supposed that he had been a fool to make a fuss about it. If he had kept his mouth shut they would not have locked him up. He should have been as subtle and as shrewd as they, kept his eyes and ears open and learned the details of and the reasons for the plot against him. He might have learned how to circumvent it.

But what if they had locked him up—the whole world was an asylum and all of them his keepers.

A key scraped in the lock, and he looked up to see an attendant entering with a tray. "Here's your dinner, sir."

"Thanks, Joe," he said gently. "Just put it down."

"Movies tonight, sir," the attendant went on. "Wouldn't you like to go? Dr. Hayward said you could—"

"No, thank you. I prefer not to."

"I wish you would, sir." He noticed with amusement the persuasive intentness of the attendant's manner. "I think the doctor wants you to. It's a good movie. There's a Mickey Mouse cartoon—"

"You almost persuade me, Joe," he answered with passive agreeableness. "Mickey's trouble is the same as mine, essentially. However, I'm not going. They need not bother to hold movies tonight."

"Oh, there will be movies in any case, sir. Lots of our other guests will attend."

"Really? Is that an example of thoroughness, or are you simply keeping up the pretense in talking to me? It isn't necessary, Joe, if it's any strain on you. I *know* the game. If I don't attend, there is no point in holding movies."

He liked the grin with which the attendant answered this thrust. Was it possible that this being was created just as he appeared to be—big muscles, phlegmatic disposition, tolerant, dog-like? Or was there nothing going on behind those kind eyes, nothing but robot reflex? No, it was more likely that he was one of them, since he was so closely in attendance on him.

The attendant left and he busied himself at his supper tray, scooping up the already-cut bits of meat with a spoon, the only implement provided. He smiled again at their caution and thoroughness. No danger of that—he would not destroy this body as long as it served him in investigating the truth of the matter. There were still many different avenues of research available before taking that possibly irrevocable step.

After supper he decided to put his thoughts in better order by writing them; he obtained paper. He should start with a general statement of some underlying postulates of the credos that had been drummed into him all his "life." Life? Yes, that was a good one. He wrote:

"I am told that I was born a certain number of years ago and that I will die a similar number of years hence. Various clumsy stories have been offered me to explain to me where

I was before birth and what becomes of me after death, but they are rough lies, not intended to deceive, except as misdirection. In every other possible way the world around me assures me that I am mortal, here but a few years, and a few years hence gone completely—non-existent.

"WRONG—I am immortal. I transcend this little time axis; a seventy-year span on it is but a casual phase in my experience. Second only to the prime datum of my own existence is the emotionally convincing certainty of my own continuity. I may be a closed curve, but closed or open, I neither have a beginning nor an end. Self-awareness is not relational; it is absolute, and cannot be reached to be destroyed, or created. Memory, however, being a relational aspect of consciousness, may be tampered with and possibly destroyed.

"It is true that most religions which have been offered me teach immortality, but note the fashion in which they teach it. The surest way to lie convincingly is to tell the truth unconvincingly. They did not wish me to believe.

"Caution: Why have they tried so hard to convince me that I am going to 'die' in a few years? There must be a very important reason. I infer that they are preparing me for some sort of a major change. It may be crucially important for me to figure out their intentions about this—probably I have several years in which to reach a decision. Note: Avoid using the types of reasoning they have taught me."

The attendant was back. "Your wife is here, sir."

"Tell her to go away."

"Please, sir—Dr. Hayward is most anxious that you should see her."

"Tell Dr. Hayward that I said that he is an excellent chess player."

"Yes, sir." The attendant waited for a moment. "Then you won't see her, sir?"

"No, I won't see her."

He wandered around the room for some minutes after the attendant had left, too distrait to return to his recapitulation. By and large, they had played very decently with him since they had brought him here. He was glad that they had allowed him to have a room alone, and he certainly had more time free for contemplation than had ever been possible on the outside. To be sure, continuous effort to keep him busy and to distract him was made, but, by being stubborn, he was able to circumvent the rules and gain some hours each day for introspection.

But, damnation!—he did wish they would not persist in using Alice in their attempts to divert his thoughts. Although the intense terror and revulsion which she had inspired in him when he had first rediscovered the truth had now aged into a simple feeling of repugnance and distaste for her company, nevertheless it was emotionally upsetting to be reminded of her, to be forced into making decisions about her.

After all, she *had* been his wife for many years. Wife? What was a wife? Another soul like one's own, a complement, the other necessary pole to the couple, a sanctuary of understanding and sympathy in the boundless depths of aloneness. *That* was what he thought, what he had needed to believe and had believed fiercely for years. The yearning need for companionship of his own kind had caused him to see himself reflected in those beautiful eyes and had made him quite uncritical of occasional incongruities in her responses.

He sighed. He felt that he had sloughed off most of the typed emotional reactions which they had taught him by precept and example, but Alice had gotten under his skin, way under, and it still hurt. He had been happy—what if it had been a dope dream? They had given him an excellent, a beautiful mirror to play with—the more fool he to have looked behind it!

Wearily he turned back to his summing up.

"The world is explained in either one of two ways: the common-sense way which says that the world is pretty much as it appears to be and that ordinary human conduct and motivations are reasonable, and the religio-mystic solution which states that the world is dream stuff, unreal, insubstantial, with reality somewhere beyond.

"WRONG—both of them. The common-sense scheme has no sense to it of any sort. 'Life is short and full of trouble. Man born of woman is born to trouble as the sparks fly upward. His days are few and they are numbered. All is vanity and vexation.' Those quotations may be jumbled and incorrect, but that is a fair statement of the common-sense world-is-as-it-seems in its only possible evaluation. In such a world, human striving is about as rational as the blind dartings of a moth against a light bulb. The 'common-sense world' is a blind insanity, out of nowhere, going nowhere, to no purpose.

"As for the other solution, it appears more rational on the surface, in that it rejects the utterly irrational world of common sense. But it is not a rational solution, it is simply a flight from reality of any sort, for it refuses to believe the results of the only available direct communication between the ego and the Outside. Certainly the 'five senses' are poor enough channels of communication, but they are the only channels."

He crumpled up the paper and flung himself from the chair. Order and logic were no good—his answer was right because it smelled right. But he still did not know all the answers. Why the grand scale of the deception, countless creatures, whole continents, an enormously involved and minutely detailed matrix of insane history, insane tradition, insane culture? Why bother with more than a cell and a strait jacket?

It must be, it had to be, because it was supremely important to deceive him completely, because a lesser deception would not do. Could it be that they dare not let him suspect his real identity no matter how difficult and involved the fraud?

He had to know. In some fashion he must get behind the deception and see what went on when he was not looking. He had had one glimpse; this time he must see the actual workings, catch the puppet masters in their manipulations.

Obviously the first step must be to escape from this asylum, but to do it so craftily they would never see him, never catch up with him, not have a chance to set the stage before him. That would be hard to do. He must excel them in shrewdness and subtlety.

Once decided, he spent the rest of the evening in considering the means by which he might accomplish his purpose. It seemed almost impossible—he must get away without once being seen and remain in strict hiding. They must lose track of him completely in order that they would not know where to center their deceptions. That would mean going without food for several days. Very well—he could do it. He must not give them any warning by unusual action or manner.

The lights blinked twice. Docilely he got up and commenced preparations for bed. When the attendant looked through the peephole he was already in bed, with his face turned to the wall.

Gladness! Gladness everywhere! It was good to be with his own kind, to hear the music swelling out of every living thing, as it always had and always would—good to know that everything was living and aware of him, participating in him, as he participated in them. It was good to be, good to know the unity of many and the diversity of one. There had been one bad thought—the details escaped him—but it was gone—it had never *been;* there was no place for it.

The early-morning sounds from the adjacent ward penetrated the sleep-laden body which served him here and gradually recalled him to awareness of the hospital room. The transition was so gentle that he carried over full recollection of what he had been doing and why. He lay still, a gentle smile on his face, and savored the uncouth, but not unpleasant, languor of the body he wore. Strange that he had ever forgotten despite their tricks and stratagems. Well, now that he had recalled the key, he would quickly set things right in this odd place. He would call them in at once and announce the new order. It would be amusing to see old Glaroon's expression when he realized that the cycle had ended—

The click of the peephole and the rasp of the door being unlocked guillotined his line of thought. The morning attendant pushed briskly in with the breakfast tray and placed it on the tip table. "Morning, sir. Nice, bright day—want it in bed, or will you get up?"

Don't answer! Don't listen! Suppress this distraction! This is part of their plan— But it was too late, too late. He felt himself slipping, falling, wrenched from reality back into the fraud world in which they had kept him. It was gone, gone completely, with no single association around him to which to anchor memory. There was nothing left but the sense of heartbreaking loss and the acute ache of unsatisfied catharsis.

"Leave it where it is. I'll take care of it."

"Okey-doke." The attendant bustled out, slamming the door, and noisily locked it.

He lay quite still for a long time, every nerve end in his body screaming for relief.

At last he got out of bed, still miserably unhappy, and attempted to concentrate on his plans for escape. But the psychic wrench he had received in being recalled so suddenly from his plane of reality had left him bruised and emotionally disturbed. His mind insisted on rechewing its doubts, rather than engage in constructive thought. Was it possible that the doctor was right, that he was not alone in his miserable dilemma? Was he really simply suffering from paranoia, delusions of self-importance?

Could it be that each unit in this yeasty swarm around him was the prison of another lonely ego—helpless, blind, and speechless, condemned to an eternity of miserable loneliness? Was the look of suffering which he had brought to Alice's face a true reflection of inner torment and not simply a piece of play-acting intended to maneuver him into compliance with their plans?

A knock sounded at the door. He said, "Come in," without looking up. Their comings and goings did not matter to him.

"Dearest—" A well-known voice spoke slowly and hesitantly.

"Alice!" He was on his feet at once, and facing her. "Who let you in here?"

"Please, dear, please—I had to see you."

"It isn't fair. It isn't fair." He spoke more to himself than to her. Then: "Why did you come?"

She stood up to him with a dignity he had hardly expected. The beauty of her childlike face had been marred by line and shadow, but it shone with an unexpected courage. "I love you," she answered quietly. "You can tell me to go away, but you can't make me stop loving you and trying to help you."

He turned away from her in an agony of indecision. Could it be possible that he had misjudged her? Was there, behind that barrier of flesh and sound symbols, a spirit that truly yearned toward his? Lovers whispering in the dark—"You *do* understand, don't you?"

"Yes, dear heart, I understand."

"Then nothing that happens to us can matter, as long as we are together and understand—" Words, words, rebounding hollowly from an unbroken wall—

No, he *couldn't* be wrong! Test her again— "Why did you keep me on that job in Omaha?"

"But I didn't make you keep that job. I simply pointed out that we should think twice before—"

"Never mind. Never mind." Soft hands and a sweet face preventing him with mild stubbornness from ever doing the thing that his heart told him to do. Always with the best of intentions, the best of intentions, but always so that he had never quite managed to do the silly, unreasonable things, that *he* knew were worth while. Hurry, hurry, hurry, and strive, with an angel-faced jockey to see that you don't stop long enough to think for yourself—

"Why did you try to stop me from going back upstairs that day?"

She managed to smile although her eyes were already spilling over with tears. "I didn't know it really mattered to you. I didn't want us to miss the train."

It had been a small thing, an unimportant thing. For some reason not clear even to him he had insisted on going back upstairs to his study when they were about to leave the house for a short vacation. It was raining, and she had pointed out that there was barely enough time to get to the station. He had surprised himself and her, too, by insisting on his own way in circumstances in which he had never been known to be stubborn.

He had actually pushed her to one side and forced his way up the stairs. Even then nothing might have come of it had he not—quite unnecessarily—raised the shade of the window that faced toward the rear of the house.

It was a very small matter. It had been raining, hard, out in front. From this window the weather was clear and sunny, with no sign of rain.

He had stood there quite a long while, gazing out at the impossible sunshine and rearranging his cosmos in his mind. He re-examined long-suppressed doubts in the light of this small but totally unexplained discrepancy. Then he had turned and had found that she was standing behind him.

He had been trying ever since to forget the expression that he had surprised on her face.

"What about the rain?"

"The rain?" she repeated in a small, puzzled voice. "Why, it was raining, of course. What about it?"

"But it was *not* raining out my study window."

"What? But of course it was. I did notice the sun break through the clouds for a moment, but that was all."

"Nonsense!"

"But darling, what has the weather to do with you and me? What difference does it make whether it rains or not—to us?" She approached him timidly and slid a small hand between his arm and side. "Am I responsible for the weather?"

"I think you are. Now please go."

She withdrew from him, brushed blindly at her eyes, gulped once, then said in a voice held steady: "All right, I'll go. But remember—you *can* come home if you want to. And I'll be there if you want me." She waited a moment, then added hesitantly: "Would you . . . would you kiss me goodby?"

He made no answer of any sort, neither with voice nor eyes. She looked at him, then turned, fumbled blindly for the door, and rushed through it.

The creature he knew as Alice went to the place of assembly without stopping to change form. "It is necessary to adjourn this sequence. I am no longer able to influence his decisions."

They had expected it, nevertheless they stirred with dismay.

The Glaroon addressed the First for Manipulation. "Prepare to graft the selected memory track at once."

Then, turning to the First for Operations, the Glaroon said: "The extrapolation shows that he will tend to escape within two of his days. This sequence degenerated primarily through your failure to extend that rainfall all around him. Be advised."

"It would be simpler if we understood his motives."

"In my capacity as Dr. Hayward, I have often thought so," commented the Glaroon acidly, "but if we understood his motives, we would be part of *him*. Bear in mind the Treaty! He almost remembered."

The creature known as Alice spoke up. "Could he not have the Taj Mahal next sequence? For some reason he values it."

"You are becoming assimilated!"

"Perhaps. I am not in fear. Will he receive it?"

"It will be considered."

The Glaroon continued with orders: "Leave structures standing until adjournment. New York City and Harvard University are now dismantled. Divert him from those sectors. Move!"

We were talking about writers with pulp backgrounds a few pages ago. Here is another, James Blish, who learned his trade in the pulps of the forties, mastered all its tricks, then put them to use in totally unexpected ways. "Mistake Inside" reads exactly like a rather standard, entertaining story of time travel or alternate worlds, familiar gambits in science fiction; but be warned—it is nothing of the kind.

James Blish

MISTAKE INSIDE

This was England, two hundred years before bomb craters had become a fixed feature of the English landscape, and while the coffee house still had precedence over the pub. The fire roared, and the smoke from long clay churchwarden pipes made a blue haze through which cheerful conversation struggled.

The door swung back, and the host stood in the opening, fat hands on hips, surveying the scene contentedly. Someone, invisible in the fog, drank a slurred uproarious toast, and a glass slammed into the fireplace, where the brandy-coated fragments made a myriad of small blue flames.

"Split me if that goes not in the reckoning!" the innkeeper bellowed. A ragged chorus of derision answered him. The inn cat shot down the stairs behind him, and its shadow glided briefly over the room as it passed the fire. It was an impossibly large, dark shadow, and for a moment it blacked out several of the booths in the rear of the chamber; the close, motionless air seemed to take on a chill. Then it was gone, and the cat, apparently annoyed by the noise, vanished into the depths of a heavy chair.

The host forgot about it. He was accustomed to its sedentary tastes. It often got sat on in the after-theater hilarity. He rolled good-naturedly across the room as someone pounded on a table for him.

But the cat, this time, had not merely burrowed into the cushions. It was gone. In the chair, in a curiously transparent condition which made him nearly invisible in the uncertain light, sat a dazed, tired figure in a Twentieth-Century tux. . . .

The radio was playing a melancholy opus called "Is You Is or Is You Ain't, My Baby" as the cab turned the corner. "Here you are, sir," croaked the driver in his 3:00 A.M. voice.

The sleepy-eyed passenger's own voice was a little unreliable. "How much?"

The fare was paid and the cabby wearily watched his erstwhile customer go up the snow-covered walk between the hedges. He put the car in gear. Then he gaped and let the clutch up. The engine died with a reproachful gasp.

The late rider had staggered suddenly sidewise toward the bushes—had he been that drunk? Of course, he had only tripped and fallen out of sight; the cabby's fleeting notion that he had melted into the air was an illusion, brought on by the unchristian lateness of the hour. Nevertheless the tracks in the snow did stop rather unaccountably. The cabby swore, started his engine, and drove away, as cautiously as he had ever driven in his life.

Behind him, from the high trees in the yard, a cat released a lonely ululation on the cold, still night.

The stage was set. . . .

There is order in all confusions; but Dr. Hugh Tracy, astronomer, knew nothing of the two events recorded above when his adventure began, so he could make no attempt at integrating them. Indeed, he was in confusion enough without dragging in any stray cats. One minute he had been charging at the door of Jeremy Wright's apartment, an automatic in his hand and blind rage in his heart. As his shoulder had splintered the panel, the world had revolved once around him, like a scene-changing stunt in the movies.

The scene had changed, all right. He was not standing in Jeremy Wright's apartment at all, but in a low-roofed, dirt-floored room built of crudely shaped logs, furnished only with two antique chairs and a rickety table from which two startled men were arising. The two were dressed in leathern jerkins of a type fashionable in the early 1700's.

"I–I beg your pardon," he volunteered lamely. "I must have mixed the apartments up." He did not turn to go immediately, however, for as he thought disgustedly concerning the lengths to which some people will go to secure atmosphere, he noticed the dirty mullioned window across the room. The sight gave him a fresh turn. He might just possibly have mistaken the number of Jeremy Wright's apartment, but certainly he hadn't imagined running up several flights of stairs! Yet beyond the window he could see plainly a cheerful sunlit street.

Sunlit. The small fact that it had been 3:00 A.M. just a minute before did not help his state of mind.

"Might I ask what you're doing breaking out of my room in this fashion?" one of the queerly-costumed men demanded, glaring at Hugh. The other, a younger man, waved his hand indulgently at his friend and sat down again. "Relax, Jonathan," he said. "Can't you see he's a transportee?"

The older man stared more closely at the befuddled Dr. Tracy. "So it is," he said. "I swear, since Yero came to power again this country has been the dumping ground of half the universe. Wherever do they get such queer clothes, do you suppose?"

"Come on in," invited the other. "Tell us your story." He winked knowingly at Jonathan, and Hugh decided he did not like him.

"First," he said, "would you mind telling me something about that window?"

The two turned to follow his pointed finger. "Why, it's just an ordinary window, in that it shows what's beyond it," said the young man. "Why?"

"I wish I knew," Hugh groaned, closing his eyes and trying to remember a few childhood prayers. The only one that came to mind was something about fourteen angels which hardly fitted the situation. After a moment he looked again, this time behind him. As he had suspected, the broken door did not lead back into the hallway of the apartment building, but into a small bedchamber of decidedly pre-Restoration cast.

"Take it easy," advised Jonathan. "It's hard to get used to at first. And put that thing away—it's a weapon of some kind, I suppose. The last transportee had one that spouted a streamer of purple gas. He was a very pleasant customer. What do you shoot?"

"Metal slugs," said Hugh, feeling faintly hysterical. "Where am I, anyhow?"

"Outside."

"Outside what?"

"That's the name of the country," the man explained patiently. "My name, by the way, is Jonathan Bell, and this gentleman is Oliver Martin."

"Hugh Tracy, Ph.D., F.R.A.S.," he added automatically.

"So now I'm inside Outside, eh? How far am I from New York? I'm all mixed up."

"New York!" exclaimed Martin. "That's a new one. The last one said he was from Tir-nam-beo. At least I'd heard of that before. How did you get here, Tracy?"

"Suddenly," Tracy said succinctly. "One minute I was bashing at the door of Jeremy Wright's apartment, all set to shoot him and get my wife out of there; and then blooey!"

"Know this Wright fellow very well, or anything about him?"

"No, I've seen him once or twice, that's all. But I know Evelyn's been going to his place quite regularly while I was at the observatory."

Bell pulled a folded and badly soiled bit of paper from his breast pocket, smoothed it out on the splintery table top, and passed it to Hugh. "Look anything like this?" he asked.

"That's him! How'd you get this? Is he here somewhere?"

Bell and Martin both smiled. "It never fails," the younger man commented. "That's Yero, the ruler of this country during fall seasons. He just assumed power again three months ago. That picture comes off the town bulletin board, from a poster announcing his approaching marriage."

"Look," Hugh said desperately. "It isn't as if I didn't like your country, but I'd like to get back to my own. Isn't there some way I can manage it?"

"Sorry," Martin said. "We can't help you there. I suppose the best thing for you to do is to consult some licensed astrologer or thaumaturgist; he can tell you what to do. There are quite a few good magicians in this town—they all wind up here eventually—and one of them ought to be able to shoot you back where you belong."

"I don't put any stock in that humbug. I'm an astronomer."

"Not responsible for your superstitions. You asked for my advice, and I gave it."

"Astrologers!" Hugh groaned. "Oh, my lord!"

"However," Martin continued, "you can stay here with us for the time being. If you're an enemy of Yero, you're a friend of ours."

Hugh scratched his head. The mental picture of himself asking an astrologer for guidance did not please him.

"I suppose I'll have to make the best of this," he said finally. "Nothing like this ever happened to me before, or to anybody I've ever heard of, so I guess I'm more or less sane. Thanks for the lodging offer. Right now I'd like to go hunt up—ulp—a magician."

Bell smiled. "All right," he said, "if you get lost in the city, just ask around. They're friendly folk, and more of 'em than you think have been in your spot. Most of the shopkeepers know Bell's place. After you've wandered about a bit you'll get the layout better. Then we can discuss further plans."

Hugh wondered what kind of plans they were supposed to discuss, but he was too anxious to discover the nature of the place into which he had fallen to discuss the question further. Bell led him down a rather smelly hallway to another door, and in a moment he found himself surveying the street.

It was all incredibly confusing. The language the two had spoken was certainly modern English, yet the busy, narrow thoroughfare was just as certainly Elizabethan in design. The houses all had overhanging second stories. Through the very center of the cobbled street ran a shallow gutter in which a thin stream of swill-like liquid trickled. The bright light flooding the scene left no doubt as to its reality, and yet there was still the faint aura of question about it. The feeling was intensified when he discovered that there was no sun; the whole dome of sky was an even dazzle. It was all like a movie set, and it was a surprise to find that the houses had backs to them.

Across the street, perched comfortably in the cool shadows of a doorway, an old man slept, a tasselled nightcap hanging down over his forehead. Over his head a sign swayed: COPPERSMITH. Not ten feet away from him a sallow young man was leaning against the wall absorbed in the contents of a very modern-looking newspaper, which bore the headlines: DOWSER CONFESSES FAIRY GOLD PLANT. Lower down on the page Hugh could make out a boxed item: STILETTO KILLER FEIGNS INSANITY. In a moment, he was sure, he wouldn't have to feign it. The paper was as jarring an anachronism in the Shakespearean street scene as a six-cylinder coupe would have been.

At least he was spared having to account for any cars, though. The conventional mode of transportation was horses, it seemed. Every so often one would canter past recklessly. Their riders paid little regard to the people under their horses' hoofs and the people in their turn scattered with good-natured oaths, like any group of twentieth century pedestrians before a taxi.

As Hugh stepped off the low stone lintel he heard a breathy whistle, and turning, beheld a small red-headed urchin coming jerkily toward him. The boy was alternately whistling and calling "Here, Fleet, Fleet, Fleet! Nice doggy! Here, Fleet!" His mode of locomotion was very peculiar; he lunged mechanically from side to side or forward as if he were a machine partly out of control.

As he came closer Hugh saw that he was holding a forked stick in his hands, the foot of the Y pointing straight ahead, preceding the lad no matter where he went. On the boy's head was a conical blue cap lettered with astrological and alchemical symbols, which had sagged so as to completely cover one eye, but he seemed loath to let go of the stick to adjust it.

In a moment the boy had staggered to a stop directly before Hugh, while the rigid and quivering end of the stick went down to Hugh's shoes and began slowly to ascend. He was conscious of a regular sniffing sound.

"Better tend to that cold, son," he suggested.

"That isn't me, it's the rod," the boy said desperately. "Please, sir, have you seen a brown puppy—" At this point the stick finished its olfactory inspection of Hugh and jerked sidewise, yanking the boy after it. As the urchin disappeared still calling "Here, Fleet!" Hugh felt a faint shiver. Here was the first evidence of a working magic before his eyes, and his sober astronomer's soul recoiled from it.

A window squealed open over his head, and he jumped just in time to avoid a gush of garbage which was flung casually down toward the gutter. Thereafter he clung as close to the wall as he could, and kept beneath the overhanging second stories. Walking thus, with his eyes on the sole-punishing cobbles, deep in puzzlement, his progress was presently arrested by collision with a mountain.

When his eyes finally reached the top of it, it turned out to be a man, a great muscular thug clad in expensive blue velvet small-clothes and a scarlet cape like an eighteenth century exquisite. Was there no stopping this kaleidoscope of anachronism?

"Weah's ya mannas?" the apparition roared. "Move out!"

"What for?" Hugh replied in his austere classroom tone. "I don't care to be used as a sewage pail any more than you do."

"Ah," said the giant. "Wise guy, eh? Dunno ya bettas, eh?" There was a whistling sound as he drew a thin sword which might have served to dispatch whales. Hugh's Royal Society reserve evaporated and he clawed frantically for his automatic, but before the double murder was committed the giant lowered his weapon and bent to stare more closely at the diminutive doctor.

"Ah," he repeated. "Ya a transportee, eh?"

"I guess so," Tracy said, remembering that Martin had used the word.

"Weah ya from?"

"Brooklyn," Hugh said hopefully.

The giant shook his head. "Weah you guys think up these here names is a wonda. Well, ya dunno the customs, that's easy t'see."

He stepped aside to let Hugh pass.

"Thank you," said Hugh with a relieved sigh. "Can you tell me where I can find an astrologer?" He still could not pronounce the word without choking.

"Ummmm—most of 'em are around the squaah. Ony, juss between you an' me, buddy, I'd keep away from there till the p'rade's ova. Yero's got an orda out fa arrestin' transportees." The giant nodded pleasantly. "Watch ya step." He stalked on down the street.

Looking after him, Hugh was startled to catch a brief glimpse of a man dressed in complete dinner clothes, including top hat, crossing the street and rounding a corner. Hoping that this vision from his own age might know something significant about this screwy world, he ran after him, but lost him in the traffic. He found nothing but a nondescript and unhappy alley-cat which ran at his approach.

Discouraged, Hugh went back the way he had come and set out in search of the public square and an astrologer. As he walked, he gradually became conscious of a growing current of people moving in the same direction, a current which was swelled by additions from every street and byway they passed. There was a predominance of holiday finery, and he remembered the giant's words about a parade. Well, he'd just follow the crowd; it would make finding the square that much easier.

Curious snatches of conversation reached his ears as he plodded along. ". . . Aye, in the square, sir; one may hope that it bodes us some change. . . ." ". . . Of Yero eke, that a younge wyfe he gat his youthe agoon, and withal. . . ." ". . . An' pritnear every time dis guy toins up, yiz kin count on gittin' it in the neck. . . ." ". . . Oft Seyld Yero sceathena threatum, hu tha aethlingas ellen fremedon. . . ."

Most of the fragments were in English, but English entirely and indiscriminantly mixed as to century. Hugh wondered if the few that sounded foreign were actually so, or whether they were some Saxon or Jutish ancestor of English —or, perhaps, English as it might sound in some remote fu-

ture century. If that latter were so, then there might be other
cities in Outside where only old, modern and future French
was spoken, or Russian, or—

The concept was too complex to entertain. He remembered the giant's warning, and shook his head. This world,
despite the obvious sweating reality of the crowd around him
and the lumpy pavement beneath his feet, was still too crazy
to be anything but a phantom. He was curious to see this
Yero, who looked so inexplicably like Jeremy Wright, but
he could not take any warning of Outside very seriously.
His principal concern was to get back inside again.

As the part of the crowd which bore him along debouched
from the narrow street into a vast open space, he heard in
the distance the sound of trumpets, blowing a complicated
fanfare. A great shouting went up, but somehow it seemed
not the usual cheering of expectant parade-goers. There was
a strange undertone—perhaps of animosity? Hugh could not
tell.

In the press he found that he could move neither forward
nor back. He would have to stand where he was until the
event was over and the mob dispersed.

By craning his neck over the shoulders of those in front
of him—a procedure which, because of his small stature, involved some rather precarious teetering on tip-toe—he could
see across the square. It was surrounded on all four sides by
houses and shops, but the street which opened upon it directly opposite him was a wide one. Through it he saw a
feature of the city which the close-grouped overhanging
houses had hidden before—a feature which put the finishing
touch upon the sense of unreality and brought back once

more the suggestion of a vast set for a Merrie-England movie by a bad director.

It was a castle. Furthermore it was twice as big as any real castle ever was, and its architecture was totally out of the period of the town below it. It was out of any period. It was a modernist's dream, a Walter Gropius design come alive. The rectangular facade and flanking square pylons were vaguely reminiscent of an Egyptian temple of Amenhotep IV's time, but the whole was of bluely gleaming metal, shimmering smoothly in the even glare of the sky.

From the flat summits floated scarlet banners bearing an unreadable device. A clustered group of these pennons before the castle seemed to be moving, and by stretching his neck almost to the snapping point Hugh could see that they were being carried by horsemen who were coming slowly down the road. Ahead of them came the trumpeters, who were now entering the square, sounding their atonal tocsin.

Now the trumpeters passed abreast of him, and the crowd made a lane to let them through. Next came the bearers of the standards, two by two, holding their horses' heads high. A group of richly dressed but ruffianly retainers followed them. The whole affair reminded Hugh of a racketeer's funeral in Chicago's prohibition days. Finally came the sedan chair which bore the royal couple—and Dr. Hugh Tracy at last lost hold of his sanity. For beside the aloof, hated Yero-Jeremy in the palanquin was Evelyn Tracy.

When Hugh came back to his senses he was shouting unintelligible epithets, and several husky townsmen were holding his arms. "Easy, Bud," one of them hissed into his ear. "Haven't you ever seen him before?"

Hugh forced himself back to a semblance of calmness, and

had sense enough to say nothing of Evelyn. "Who—what is
he?" he gasped. The other looked at him tensely for a moment, then, reassured, let go of him.

"That's Yero. He's called many names, but the most common is The Enemy. Better get used to seeing him. You can't
help hating him, but it'll do you no good to fly off the handle
like that."

"You mean everybody hates him?"

The townsman frowned. "Why certainly. He's The
Enemy."

"Then why don't you throw him out?"

"Well—"

The other burgher, who had said nothing thus far, broke
in: "Presenuk prajolik solda, soldama mera per ladsua hrut-
kai; per stanisch felemetskje droschnovar."

"Exactly," said the other man. "You okay now, Bud?"

"Ulp," Hugh said. "Yes, I'm all right."

The crowd, still roaring its ambiguous cheer, was following
the procession out the other end of the square, and shortly
Hugh found himself standing almost alone. A sign over a
nearby shop caught his eye: *Dr. ffoni, Licensed Magician.*
Here was what he had been looking for. As he ran quickly
across the square toward the rickety building he thought he
caught a glimpse out of the tail of his eyes of a top hat moving along in the departing crowd, but he dismissed it. That
could wait.

The shop was dark inside, and at first he thought it empty.
But in answer to repeated shouts a scrambling began in the
back room, and a nondescript little man entered, struggling
into a long dark gown several sizes too large for him.

"Sorry," he puffed, trying to regain his right hand, which

he had lost down the wrong sleeve, "out watching the parade. May I serve you, young sir?"

"Yes. I'm a transportee, and I'd like to get back where I belong."

"So would we all, so would we all, indeed," said the magician, nodding vigorously. "Junior!"

"Yes, paw." A gawky adolescent peered out of the back room.

"Customer."

"Ah, paw. I don' wanna go in t' any trance. I'm dragging a rag-bag to a rat-race t'night an' I wanna be groovy. You know prognostics allus knock me flatter'n a mashed-potato san'witch."

"You'll do as you're told, or I'll not allow you to use the broomstick. You see, young sir," the magician addressed Hugh, "familiar spirits are at somewhat of a premium around here, there being so many in this town in my profession; but since my wife was a Sybil, my son serves me adequately in commissions of this nature."

He turned back to the boy, who was now sitting on a stool behind the counter, and produced a pink lollipop from the folds of his robe. The boy allowed it to be placed in his mouth docilely enough, and closed his eyes. Hugh watched, not knowing whether to laugh or to swear. If this idiotic procedure produced results, he was sure he'd never be able to contemplate Planck's Constant seriously again.

"Now then, while we're waiting," the sorcerer continued, "you should understand the situation. All living has two sides, the IN-side and the OUT-side. The OUT-side is where the roots of significant mistakes are embedded; the IN-side where they flower. Since most men have their backs turned to the OUT-side all their lives, few mistakes can be rectified.

But if a man turns, as if on a pivot, so that he faces the other way, he may see and be on the OUT-side, and have the opportunity to uproot his error if he can find the means. Such a fortunate man is a transportee."

"So, in effect, existence has just been given a half-turn around me, to put me facing outside instead of inside where I belong?"

"A somewhat egotistical way of putting it, but that is the general idea. The magicians of many ages have used this method of disposing of their enemies; for unless the transportee can find his Avatars—the symbols, as it were, of his error—and return them to their proper places, he must remain Outside forever. This last many have done by choice, since none ever dies Outside."

"I'd just as soon not," Hugh said with a groan. "What are my Avatars?"

"To turn a capstan there must be a lever, and to pivot a man Outside means that two other living beings must act as the ends of this lever, and exchange places in time. Your Avatars changed places in time, while you stood still in time and space, but were pivoted to face Outside."

At this point he reached over to the boy and gave an experimental tug on the protruding stick of the lollipop. It slipped out easily; all the pink candy had dissolved. "Ah," he said. "We are about ready." He made a few passes with his hands and began to sing:

"Jet propulsion, Dirac hole,
"Trochilminthes, Musterole,
"Plenum, bolide, Ding an sich,
"Shoot the savvy to me, Great White Which!"

The tune was one more commonly associated with Pepsi-Cola. After a moment the boy's mouth opened, and licking the remains of the lollipop from its corners, he said clearly, "Two hundred. Night prowlers."

"Is that all?" Hugh said, not much surprised.

"That's quite enough. Well, maybe not quite enough, but it's about all I ever get."

"But what does it mean?"

"Why, simply this: that your Avatars are two hundred years apart from each other; and that they are night-prowlers."

"Two hundred years! And I have to find them?"

"They are represented by simulacra in Outside. You must identify these simulacra and touch each one; this done, they will exchange again, and you will be rotated Inside. Have you seen any here?"

A light burst in Hugh's brain. "I saw a man from my own age who looked like a bona-fide night-prowler all right."

"You see?" The magician spread his hands expressively. "Half the work is over. Simply search for another night-prowler whose costume is two hundred years older—or, of course, younger—than the first. It's very simple. Now, young sir—" The hands began to wash each other suggestively.

Hugh produced a handful of coins. "That's no good," said the little man with a sniff. "I can make that myself. It's the city's principal industry. I don't suppose you have any sugar on you? Or rubber bands? No? Hmm. How about that?"

He prodded Hugh's vest. "That" was Hugh's Sigma Chi key, dangling from his watch chain. He had been elected to the honorary society by virtue of a closely reasoned paper on the deficiencies of current stellar evolution hypotheses. With a grin he passed it across the counter. "Thanks," the thaumaturgist said, "I collect fetishes. Totem fixation, I guess."

Feeling rather humble, Hugh left the shop and started back toward Bell's house by the most direct route his memory could provide. Now that he had begun to get his bearings, his stomach was reminding him that he had gone the whole day without food. On the way he saw the known Avatar half-way down a dark alley, contemplating a low doorway sorrowfully; but when he arrived, the top-hatted figure was gone. By the time he entered the house where he had had his first glimpse of Outside, he was decidedly discouraged, but the pleasant smell of food revived him somewhat.

"Good evening," Bell greeted him, though the ambiguous daylight was as unvaryingly bright as ever. "Find your astrologer?"

"Yes. Now I have to find a night-prowler. You wouldn't be one, by any chance?"

The man laughed softly. "In a sense, yes, but I'm too old to be the one you want. You're Avatar-hunting, I take it?"

"That's it."

"Well, I'm not a simulacrum. I'm a native here, one of the original settlers. Come on and eat, anyhow." He led the way into the room which Hugh had first seen, and waved him to the table. On it was a platter bearing a complete roast hog's head with an apple in its mouth and three strips of bacon between its ears, a pudding, a meat pie, a spitted duckling, three wooden trenchers—boards used as plates—and three razor-sharp knives. Obviously forks were not in style Outside.

"Has Yero's administration caused a potato shortage?" Hugh asked curiously.

"Potato? No. You transportees have odd ideas; you mean potatoes to eat? Don't you know they're a relative of the deadly nightshade?"

Hugh shrugged and fell to. There was bread anyhow. During the course of the meal the two pumped him about his experiences during the day, and he answered with increasing caution. They seemed to be up to something. He especially disliked young Martin, whose knowing smile when Hugh described his belief that Yero's queen was in actuality his own wife irritated him. As the dinner ended Bell came to the point.

"You've heard Yero spoken of as The Enemy? Well, his rule here is intermittent. He just pops up every fall season and takes the place of the Old One, who is the only rightful king, and a good one. It's during Yero's ascendancy that all the transportees show up—all the people who make mistakes during that period, if the mistakes are of a certain kind, get pivoted around here to correct them. It gets pretty nuisancy.

"You can see what I mean. Here you come busting in on us and split our good pine door and eat one third of our food. Not that we begrudge you the food; you're welcome to it; but it is a bother to have all these strangers around. In addition it decreases the future population in a way I haven't time to describe now. Everybody hates Yero, even the transportees. It's our idea to assassinate him before he gets to come back another time; then the Old One can really do us some good and the town can come back to normal. Sounds reasonable, doesn't it?"

"I thought no one ever died here."

"Nobody ever does, naturally, but accidents or violence can distribute an individual to the point of helplessness. Since you seem to hate Yero like the rest of us, we thought you might like to throw in with us."

The hospitality of the two did not permit him to refuse immediately, but more and more he was sure he did not want to be involved in any project of theirs. Bell's picture of what Outside's substitute for death was like revolted him; and in addition, the thought occurred to him that it would be dangerous to take any positive steps while he was still ignorant of the error that had brought him here.

"I'd like to sleep on that," he said cautiously. "Do you mind if I defer judgment for the night? I haven't had any sleep for thirty-six hours, and I'll just pass out, if I don't get some."

"All right," Bell said. "You think it over. With The Enemy out of the way it might be easier to find your Avatars, too, you know. Nothing ever works right while he's in power."

When Hugh awoke his brain did not function properly for quite a few seconds. The bed had had fleas in it, and the changeless brilliancy of the "daylight" had kept him awake a long time despite his exhaustion. The sight of the black-clad figure seated on the nearby stool did not register at first.

"Good mornin'," he said muzzily. Then, "You!"

"Me," the man in the top hat replied ungrammatically. "I

had to wait for the two Princes to get out of the house before I could see you. I've been looking for you."

"*You've* been looking for *me*," Hugh repeated angrily, sitting up in bed. He noticed with only faint surprise that the wall of the room was plainly visible through the visitant's shirt bosom. "Well, you'll have to solidify a minute if you're going to do me any good. I'm supposed to touch you."

"Not yet. When you do, this image will vanish, and I've got a few things to talk to you about before that happens. I got bounced back two hundred years in time past on account of a fool mistake you made, and I'm as anxious to see you straightened out as you are yourself." He hiccuped convulsively. "Luckily I'm a book collector with a special bent towards Cruikshank. I had sense enough to consult Dr. Lee while I was behind the times, and found out where you were. Do you know?"

"Where am I? Why, I'm Outside."

"Use your noggin. How much does 'Outside' mean to you, anyhow?"

"Very little," Hugh agreed. "Well, the only other place I know where people go that make mistakes is—awk! Now, wait a minute! Don't tell me—"

The figure nodded solemnly. "Now you've got it. You should have guessed that when the Princes told you their boss was called the Old One. You've already had clue after clue that they're forbidden to conceal from you; that no one dies here; that all the world's magicians come here eventually; that making money—remember the saying about the root of all evil?—is the town's principal industry; and so on."

"Well, well." Hugh scratched his head. "Hugh Tracy, Ph.D., F.R.A.S., spending a season in Hell just like Rimbaud or some other crazy poet. The fall season at that. How Evelyn would love this. But it's not quite as I would have pictured it."

"Why should it have been?"

Hugh could think of no answer. "Who's Yero, then? He's called The Enemy."

"He's their enemy, sure enough. I don't know exactly who he is, but he's someone in authority, and his job is to see the Purgatory candidates get a chance to straighten things out for themselves. Naturally the Fallen buck him as much as possible; and part of the trick is to disguise the place somewhat, to keep its nature hidden from the transportees—the potential damned—and lure them into doing something that will keep them here for good. That bed you're in, for instance, is probably a pool of flaming brimstone or something of the sort."

Hugh bounded out hastily.

"Yero establishes himself in the fortress of Dis, which is what that pile of chromium junk is, up on the hill, after you get behind the disguise. Each time he comes, he makes a tour through the town, showing himself to each newcomer in a form which will mean the most to that person. The important thing is that few people take kindly to being corrected in the fundamental kinds of mistakes that bring them here, so that nine times out of ten Yero's appearance to you makes you hate him."

"Hmm," Hugh said. "I begin to catch on, around the edges, as it were. To me he looked like a man I'd started out to murder a few days ago."

"You're on the track. Examine your motives, use your head, son, and don't let the Princes trick you into anything." The pellucid shape steadied and grew real and solid by degrees; the man in the top hat rose and walked toward the bed. "Above all—don't hate Yero."

His outstretched hand touched Hugh's sleeve, and he vanished on the instant with a sharp hiccup.

There was no one in the house, and nothing to eat but a half-consumed and repellent-looking pudding left over from the "night" before, which he finished for lack of anything else rather than out of any attraction the suety object had as a breakfast dish. Then he left the house in search of the other Avatar.

The light was bright and cheerful as always, but he felt chilly all the same. Discovering where he was had destroyed all of his amusement in the town's crazy construction, and taken the warmth out of his bones. He eyed the passers-by uneasily, wondering as each one approached him whether he was seeing someone like himself, a soul in eternal torment, or an emissary of the Fallen whose real form was ambiguous.

For the rest of the morning he roamed the streets in search of a likely-looking figure, but finally he had to admit that his wanderings were fruitless. He sat down on a doorstep to think it out.

His Avatars were the "symbols of his error"; they were night-prowlers, obviously, because he had been one himself, gun in hand. The error itself was something to do with Jeremy Wright and Evelyn—not the impending murder, because it had not been committed, but some other error. The man in the top hat had been chosen, perhaps, because he had conceived of Wright as a cavalier, a suave home-breaker, or something of the sort; dinner clothes made a pointed symbol of such a notion. Of what else, specifically, had he suspected Jeremy? Tom-catting!

He groaned and dropped his head in his hands, remembering the cat he had seen in conjunction with his first sight of the man in dinner clothes. How was he to find one ragged alley-cat in a town where there were doubtless hundreds? Cats did not wear period costumes. He couldn't go around touching cats until something happened!

He heard a sniffing sound and a thin mournful whine at his side. He looked down.

"Go 'way," he said. "I want a cat, not a mongrel pooch."

The puppy, recoiling at the unfriendly tone, dropped its tail and began to sidle away from him, and gloomily he watched it go. Brown dog?—Brown cat?—Brown dog! An inspiration!

"Here, Fleet," he essayed. The puppy burst into a frenzy of tail-wagging and came back, with that peculiar angled trot only dogs out of all the four-footed beasts seem to affect. Hugh patted its head, and it whined and licked his hand.

"There, there," he said. "You're lost, I know. So am I. If your name is Fleet, we'll both be home shortly. It darn well better be Fleet."

Hugh considered the animal speculatively. It certainly seemed to respond to the name; but then, it was only a puppy, and might just as easily respond to any friendly noise. Grimly he sat and waited. In about an hour the dog began to get restless, and Hugh carted it across the street to a shop and bought it some meat, leaving in payment a letter from a colleague which the shopkeeper seemed to think was full of cantrips, charms of some kind. Then he resumed his vigil.

It was approximately four o'clock by his personal time-keeping system when he finally heard the sound he had been listening for, but not daring to expect—the voice of the red-headed urchin, calling his dog's name in incredibly weary tones. In a moment the boy appeared, his face tear-streaked, his feet stumbling, his eyes heavy from lack of sleep. The stick was still pulling him, and the conical cap, by a miracle, still rested askew on his head. The rod lunged forward eagerly as soon as it pointed toward Hugh, and the boy stopped by the doorstep, the divining rod pointing in quivering triumph squarely at the puppy. The boy sat down in the street and began to bawl.

"Now, now," said Hugh. "You've found your dog. Don't cry. What's the matter?"

"I haven't had any sleep or any food," the boy snuffled. "I couldn't let go, and the dog could move faster than I could, so I've been pulled all over the city, and I'll bet it's all the Old One's fault, too—" His voice rose rapidly and Hugh tried to calm him down, a little abstractedly, for in the reference to the Old One, Hugh had recognized the boy's real nature, and knew him for an ally. Wait till I tell Evelyn, he told himself, that I've seen an Archangel and one of the Cherubim face to face, and hatched plots with the Fallen!

"I saw your dog, and figured probably you'd be along."

"Oh, thank you, sir. I guess I'd have spent the rest of eternity chasing him if you hadn't held him until I could catch up with him." He looked angrily at the forked stick, which now lay inert and innocuous on the cobbled pavement. "I used the wrong spell, and it had to smell people. No wonder we could never get close enough to Fleet for him to hear me!"

"Do you think you could make the rod work again?"

"Oh, yes, sir. Only I never would."

"I want to use it. Do you mind?"

"I don't mind. It's my uncle's, but I can always cut another one. Only it won't work without the hat, and I took that from my uncle too. He's an Authority," the urchin added proudly. Hugh thought of Goethe's Sorcerer's Apprentice and grinned.

"How come you didn't shake your head and knock it off when you got tired?"

"Oh, the hat only starts it. After that it goes by itself. I just didn't want to lose my uncle's hat, that's all."

"Good for you. Then suppose I borrow the hat for just a minute, and you grab it when the stick starts. I want to find a cat."

The boy shook his head doubtfully. "I wouldn't want to do it myself, but it's your business. What kind of cat? I have to make up a spell."

Hugh anticipated some difficulty in explaining what it was he wanted, but to his relief the boy had already recognized him as a transportee and understood at once.

"All right. Put the hat on. Pick up the stick like I had it. That's it, one fork in each hand. Now then:

"Seeker of souls, lost boys and girls,
"Of objects and of wells,
"Find his gate between the worlds
"Before the curfew knells;

"Find the cat who should reside
"In the mortal world Inside."

The divining rod started forward with a terrific jerk, and Hugh plunged after it. The boy ran alongside him and snatched off the magician's cap. "Thanks," Hugh shouted. "You're welcome," the boy called after him. "Good luck, sir, and thank you for holding my dog." Then the stick hauled Hugh around a corner, and the dog-owner was gone; but in Hugh's mind there remained a split-second glimpse of a strange smile, mischievous, kindly, and agelessly wise.

The cherub had not specified in his incantation which sense the rod was to use, and so it had chosen the quickest one—intuition, or supersensory-perception, or sixth-sense— Hugh had heard it called many things, but until he held the ends of the fork he had never quite comprehended what it was.

The stick drew him faster. His toes seemed barely to touch the hard cobbles. Almost it seemed as if he were about to fly. Yet, somehow, there was no wind in his face, nor any real sensation of speed. All about him was a breathless quiet, an intent hush of light through which he soared. The houses and shops of the town sped by him, blurred and sadly unreal. The outlines danced waveringly in a haze of heat.

The town was changing.

Fear lodged a prickly lump in his larynx. The facades were going down as he came closer to his own world. He knew that before long the conventional disguises of the town would be melted, and Hell would begin to show through. Startled faces turned to watch him as he passed, and their features were not as they should be. Once he was sure he had confronted Bell and Martin for an instant.

A cry, distant and wild, went up behind him. It had been Bell—or was it—Belial? Other feet were running beside his own; shortly there were other cries, and then a gathering roar and tumult of voices; the street began to throb dully with the stampeding feet of a great mob. The rod yanked him down an alleyway. The thunder followed.

In the unreal spaces of the public square the other entrances were already black with blurred figures howling down upon him. The stick did not falter, but rushed headlong toward the castle. His hands sweated profusely on the fork, and his feet skimmed the earth in great impossible bounds. The gates of the fortress swept toward him. There were shadowy guards there, but they were looking through him at the mob behind; the next instant he was passing them.

The mists of unreality became thick, translucent. Everything around him was a vague reddish opalescence through which the sounds of the herd rioted, seemingly from every direction. Suddenly he was sure he was surrounded; but the rod arrowed forward regardless, and he had to follow.

At last the light began to coalesce, and in a moment he saw floating before him a shining crystal globe, over which floated the illuminated faces of his wife—and—Yero, The Enemy. This was the crucial instant, and he remembered the simulacrum's advice: "Don't hate Yero."

Indeed, he could not. He had nearly forgotten whom it

was that Yero resembled, so great was his desire for escape, and his fear of the tumult behind him.

The light grew, and by it, the table upon which the crystal rested, and the bodies belonging to the two illuminated heads, became slowly visible. There was a cat there, too; he saw the outline become sharp as he catapulted on through the dimness. He tried to slow down as he approached the table. The rod, this time, did not resist. The two heads regarded him with slow surprise. The cat began to rise and bristle.

The shouting died.

"Hugh!"

He was in Jeremy Wright's apartment, a splintered door behind him, his heels digging into the carpet to halt his headlong charge. In his outstretched hand was, not a warped divining rod, but a gun.

"Hugh!" his wife cried again. "You found out! But—"

The table was still there, and the crystal. The cat and the castle were gone. But Jeremy Wright was still dressed in the robes of an astrologer. He *was* an astrologer.

"I'm sorry, darling, honestly—I knew you hated it, but— after all, breaking in this way! And—a gun! After all, even if you *do* think it's humbug—"

Hugh looked at the serene face of Jeremy Wright, and silently pocketed the automatic. There was nothing, after all, that he could have said to either of them.

H. L. Gold, who founded *Galaxy* in 1950, is warmly remembered for his contributions, ten years earlier, to the magazine *Unknown*. John Campbell's *Unknown* was the first magazine in the world entirely devoted to modern fantasy —stories, like those in this book, in which the fantastic premise is explored as logically and realistically as in good science fiction—and Gold was one of the handful of writers who shaped the magazine and established its pattern.

This story, to my mind, is a minor classic. The "water gnome" is a weak invention, not meant to be taken seriously, but the people are real. Gold has said that Greenberg's misadventures were not funny to him when he wrote the story; I think that may be one of the secrets of high comedy.

H. L. Gold

TROUBLE
WITH WATER

Greenberg did not deserve his surroundings. He was the first fisherman of the season, which guaranteed him a fine catch; he sat in a dry boat—one without a single leak—far out on a lake that was ruffled only enough to agitate his artificial fly. The sun was warm, the air was cool; he sat comfortably on a cushion; he had brought a hearty lunch; and two bottles of beer hung over the stern in the cold water.

Any other man would have been soaked with joy to be fishing on such a splendid day. Normally, Greenberg himself would have been ecstatic, but instead of relaxing and waiting for a nibble, he was plagued by worries.

This short, slightly gross, definitely bald, eminently respectable businessman lived a gypsy life. During the summer he lived in a hotel with kitchen privileges in Rockaway; winters he lived in a hotel with kitchen privileges in Florida; and in both places he operated concessions. For years now, rain had fallen on schedule every weekend, and there had been storms and floods on Decoration Day, July 4th and Labor Day. He did not love his life, but it was a way of making a living.

He closed his eyes and groaned. If he had only had a son instead of his Rosie! Then things would have been mighty different—

For one thing, a son could run the hot dog and hamburger griddle, Esther could draw beer, and he would make soft drinks. There would be small difference in the profits, Greenberg admitted to himself; but at least those profits could be put aside for old age, instead of toward a dowry for his miserably ugly, dumpy, pitifully eager Rosie.

"All right—so what do I care if she don't get married?" he had cried to his wife a thousand times. "I'll support her. Other men can set up boys in candy stores with soda fountains that have only two spigots. Why should I have to give a boy a regular International Casino?"

"May your tongue rot in your head, you no-good piker!" she would scream. "It ain't right for a girl to be an old maid. If we have to die in the poorhouse, I'll get my poor Rosie a husband. Every penny we don't need for living goes to her dowry!"

Greenberg did not hate his daughter, nor did he blame her for his misfortunes; yet, because of her, he was fishing with a broken rod that he had to tape together.

That morning his wife opened her eyes and saw him packing his equipment. She instantly came awake. "Go ahead!" she shrilled—speaking in a conversational tone was not one of her accomplishments—"Go fishing, you loafer! Leave me here alone. I can connect the beer pipes and the gas for soda water. I can buy ice cream, frankfurters, rolls, syrup, and watch the gas and electric men at the same time. Go ahead—go fishing!"

"I ordered everything," he mumbled soothingly. "The gas and electric won't be turned on today. I only wanted to go fishing—it's my last chance. Tomorrow we open the concession. Tell the truth, Esther, can I go fishing after we open?"

"I don't care about that. Am I your wife or ain't I, that you should go ordering everything without asking me—"

He defended his actions. It was a tactical mistake. While she was still in bed, he should have picked up his equipment and left. By the time the argument got around to Rosie's dowry, she stood facing him.

"For myself I don't care," she yelled. "What kind of a monster are you that you can go fishing while your daughter eats her heart out? And on a day like this yet! You should only have to make supper and dress Rosie up. A lot you care that a nice boy is coming to supper tonight and maybe take Rosie out, you no-good father, you!"

From that point it was only one hot protest and a shrill curse to find himself clutching half a broken rod, with the other half being flung at his head.

Now he sat in his beautifully dry boat on a excellent game lake far out on Long Island, desperately aware that any average fish might collapse his taped rod.

What else could he expect? He had missed his train; he had had to wait for the boathouse proprietor; his favorite dry fly was missing; and, since morning, not a fish struck at the bait. Not a single fish!

And it was getting late. He had no more patience. He ripped the cap off a bottle of beer and drank it, in order to gain courage to change his fly for a less sporting blood-worm. It hurt him, but he wanted a fish.

The hook and the squirming worm sank. Before it came to rest, he felt a nibble. He sucked in his breath exultantly and snapped the hook deep into the fish's mouth. Sometimes, he thought philosophically, they just won't take artificial bait. He reeled in slowly.

"Oh, Lord," he prayed, "a dollar for charity—just don't let the rod bend in half where I taped it!"

It was sagging dangerously. He looked at it unhappily and raised his ante to five dollars; even at that price it looked impossible. He dipped his rod into the water, parallel with the line, to remove the strain. He was glad no one could see him do it. The line reeled in without a fight.

"Have I—God forbid!—got an eel or something not kosher?" he mumbled. "A plague on you—why don't you fight?"

He did not really care what it was—even an eel—anything at all.

He pulled in a long, pointed, brimless green hat.

For a moment he glared at it. His mouth hardened. Then, viciously, he yanked the hat off the hook, threw it on the floor and trampled on it. He rubbed his hands together in anguish.

"All day I fish," he wailed, "two dollars for train fare, a dollar for a boat, a quarter for bait, a new rod I got to buy—and a five-dollar-mortgage charity has got on me. For what? For you, you hat, you!"

Out in the water an extremely civil voice asked politely: "May I have my hat, please?"

Greenberg glowered up. He saw a little man come swimming vigorously through the water toward him; small arms crossed with enormous dignity, vast ears on a pointed face propelling him quite rapidly and efficiently. With serious determination he drove through the water, and, at the starboard rail, his amazing ears kept him stationary while he looked gravely at Greenberg.

"You are stamping on my hat," he pointed out without anger.

To Greenberg this was highly unimportant. "With the ears you're swimming," he grinned in a superior way. "Do you look funny!"

"How else could I swim?" the little man asked politely.

"With the arms and legs, like a regular human being, of course."

"But I am not a human being. I am a water gnome, a relative of the more common mining gnome. I cannot swim with my arms, because they must be crossed to give an appearance of dignity suitable to a water gnome; and my feet are used for writing and holding things. On the other hand, my ears are perfectly adapted for propulsion in water. Consequently, I employ them for that purpose. But please, my hat—there are several matters requiring my immediate attention, and I must not waste time."

Greenberg's unpleasant attitude toward the remarkably civil gnome is easily understandable. He had found someone he could feel superior to, and, by insulting him, his depressed ego could expand. The water gnome certainly looked inoffensive enough, being only two feet tall.

"What you got that's so important to do, Big Ears?" he asked nastily.

Greenberg hoped the gnome would be offended. He was not, since his ears, to him, were perfectly normal, just as you would not be insulted if a member of a race of atrophied beings were to call you "Big Muscles." You might even feel flattered.

"I really must hurry," the gnome said, almost anxiously. "But if I have to answer your questions in order to get back my hat—we are engaged in re-stocking the Eastern waters with fish. Last year there was quite a drain. The bureau of fisheries is co-operating with us to some extent, but, of course, we cannot depend too much on them. Until the population rises to normal, every fish has instructions not to nibble."

Greenberg allowed himself a smile, an annoyingly skeptical smile.

"My main work," the gnome went on resignedly, "is control of the rainfall over the Eastern seaboard. Our fact-finding committee, which is scientifically situated in the meteorological center of the continent, co-ordinates the rainfall needs of the entire continent; and when they determine the amount of rain needed in particular spots of the East, I make it rain to that extent. Now may I have my hat, please?"

Greenberg laughed coarsely. "The first lie was big enough —about telling the fish not to bite. You make it rain like I'm President of the United States!" He bent toward the gnome slyly. "How's about proof?"

"Certainly, if you insist." The gnome raised his patient, triangular face toward a particularly clear blue spot in the sky, a trifle to one side of Greenberg. "Watch that bit of the sky."

Greenberg looked up humorously. Even when a small dark cloud rapidly formed in the previously clear spot, his grin remained broad. It could have been coincidental. But then large drops of undeniable rain fell over a twenty-foot circle; and Greenberg's mocking grin shrank and grew sour.

He glared hatred at the gnome, finally convinced. "So you're the dirty crook who makes it rain on weekends!"

"Usually on weekends during the summer," the gnome admitted. "Ninety-two percent of water consumption is on weekdays. Obviously we must replace that water. The weekends, of course, are the logical time."

"But, you thief!" Greenberg cried hysterically. "You murderer! What do you care what you do to my concession with your rain? It ain't bad enough business would be rotten even without rain, you got to make floods!"

"I'm sorry," the gnome replied, untouched by Greenberg's rhetoric. "We do not create rainfall for the benefit of men. We are here to protect the fish.

"Now please give me my hat. I have wasted enough time, when I should be preparing the extremely heavy rain needed for this coming weekend."

Greenberg jumped to his feet in the unsteady boat. "Rain this weekend—when I can maybe make a profit for a change! A lot you care if you ruin business. May you and your fish die a horrible, lingering death!"

And he furiously ripped the green hat to pieces and hurled them at the gnome.

"I'm really sorry you did that," the little fellow said calmly, his huge ears treading water without the slightest increase of pace to indicate his anger. "We Little Folk have no tempers to lose. Nevertheless, occasionally we find it necessary to discipline certain of your people, in order to retain our dignity. I am not malignant; but, since you hate water and those who live in it, water and those who live in it will keep away from you."

With his arms still folded in great dignity, the tiny water gnome flipped his vast ears and disappeared in a neat surface dive.

Greenberg glowered at the spreading circles of waves. He did not grasp the gnome's final restraining order; he did not even attempt to interpret it. Instead he glared angrily out of the corner of his eye at the phenomenal circle of rain that fell from a perfectly clear sky. The gnome must have remembered it at length, for a moment later the rain stopped. Like shutting off a faucet, Greenberg unwillingly thought.

"Goodby, weekend business," he growled. "If Esther finds out I got into an argument with the guy who makes it rain—"

He made an underhand cast, hoping for just one fish. The line flew out over the water; then the hook arched upward and came to rest several inches above the surface, hanging quite steadily and without support in the air.

"Well, go down in the water, damn you!" Greenberg said viciously, and he swished his rod back and forth to pull the hook down from its ridiculous levitation. It refused.

Muttering something incoherent about being hanged before he'd give in, Greenberg hurled his useless rod at the water. By this time he was not surprised when it hovered in the air above the lake. He merely glanced red-eyed at it, tossed out the remains of the gnome's hat, and snatched up the oars.

When he pulled back on them to row to land, they did not touch the water—naturally. Instead they flashed unimpeded through the air, and Greenberg tumbled into the bow.

"A-ha!" he grated. "Here's where the trouble begins." He

bent over the side. As he had suspected, the keel floated a remarkable distance above the lake.

By rowing against the air, he moved with maddening slowness toward shore, like a medieval conception of a flying machine. His main concern was that no one should see him in his humiliating position.

At the hotel he tried to sneak past the kitchen to the bathroom. He knew that Esther waited to curse him for fishing the day before opening, but more especially on the very day that a nice boy was coming to see her Rosie. If he could dress in a hurry, she might have less to say—

"Oh, there you are, you good-for-nothing!"

He froze to a halt.

"Look at you!" she screamed shrilly. "Filthy—you stink from fish!"

"I didn't catch anything, darling," he protested timidly.

"You stink anyhow. Go take a bath, may you drown in it! Get dressed in two minutes or less, and entertain the boy when he gets here. Hurry!"

He locked himself in, happy to escape her voice, started the water in the tub, and stripped from the waist up. A hot bath, he hoped, would rid him of his depressed feeling.

First, no fish; now, rain on weekends! What would Esther say—if she knew, of course. And, of course, he would not tell her.

"Let myself in for a lifetime of curses!" he sneered. "Ha!"

He clamped a new blade into his razor, opened the tube of shaving cream, and stared objectively at the mirror. The dominant feature of the soft, chubby face that stared back was its ugly black stubble; but he set his stubborn chin and glowered. He really looked quite fierce and indomitable. Unfortunately, Esther never saw his face in that uncharacteristic pose, otherwise she would speak more softly.

"Herman Greenberg never gives in!" he whispered between savagely hardened lips. "Rain on weekends, no fish—anything he wants; a lot I care! Believe me, he'll come crawling to me before I go to him."

He gradually became aware that his shaving brush was not getting wet. When he looked down and saw the water dividing into streams that flowed around it, his determined face slipped and grew desperately anxious. He tried to trap the water—by catching it in his cupped hands, by creeping up on it from behind, as if it were some shy animal, and shoving his brush at it—but it broke and ran away from his touch. Then he jammed his palm against the faucet. Defeated, he heard it gurgle back down the pipe, probably as far as the main.

"What do I do now?" he groaned. "Will Esther give it to me if I don't take a shave! But how? . . . I can't shave without water."

Glumly, he shut off the bath, undressed and stepped into the tub. He lay down to soak. It took a moment of horrified stupor to realize that he was completely dry and that he lay in a waterless bathtub. The water, in one surge of revulsion, had swept out onto the floor.

"Herman, stop splashing!" his wife yelled. "I just washed that floor. If I find one little puddle I'll murder you!"

Greenberg surveyed the instep-deep pool over the bathroom floor. "Yes, my love," he croaked unhappily.

With an inadequate washrag he chased the elusive water, hoping to mop it all up before it could seep through to the apartment below. His washrag remained dry, however, and he knew that the ceiling underneath was dripping. The water was still on the floor.

In despair, he sat on the edge of the bathtub. For some time he sat in silence. Then his wife banged on the door, urging him to come out. He started and dressed moodily.

When he sneaked out and shut the bathroom door tightly on the flood inside, he was extremely dirty and his face was raw where he had experimentally attempted to shave with a dry razor.

"Rosie!" he called in a hoarse whisper. "Sh! Where's Mamma?"

His daughter sat on a studio couch and applied nail polish to her stubby fingers. "You look terrible," she said in a conversational tone. "Aren't you going to shave?"

He recoiled at the sound of her voice, which, to him, roared out like a siren. "Quiet, Rosie! Sh!" And for further emphasis, he shoved his lips out against a warning finger. He heard his wife striding heavily around the kitchen. "Rosie," he cooed. "I'll give you a dollar if you'll mop up the water I spilled in the bathroom."

"I can't, Papa," she stated firmly. "I'm all dressed."

"Two dollars, Rosie—all right, two and a half, you blackmailer."

He flinched when he heard her gasp in the bathroom; but, when she came out with soaked shoes, he fled downstairs. He wandered aimlessly toward the village.

Now he was in for it, he thought; screams from Esther, tears from Rosie—plus a new pair of shoes for Rosie and two and a half dollars. It would be worse, though, if he could not get rid of his whiskers—

Rubbing the tender spots where his dry razor had raked his face, he mused blankly at a drugstore window. He saw nothing to help him, but he went inside anyhow and stood hopefully at the drug counter. A face peered at him through a space scratched in the wall case mirror, and the druggist came out. A nice-looking, intelligent fellow, Greenberg saw at a glance.

"What you got for shaving that I can use without water?" he asked.

"Skin irritation, eh?" the pharmacist replied. "I got something very good for that."

"No. It's just— Well, I don't like to shave with water."

The druggist seemed disappointed. "Well, I got brushless shaving cream." Then he brightened. "But I got an electric razor—much better."

"How much?" Greenberg asked cautiously.

"Only fifteen dollars, and it lasts a lifetime."

"Give me the shaving cream," Greenberg said coldly.

With the tactical science of a military expert, he walked around until some time after dark. Only then did he go back to the hotel, to wait outside. It was after seven, he was getting hungry, and the people who entered the hotel he knew as permanent summer guests. At last a stranger passed him and ran up the stairs.

Greenberg hesitated for a moment. The stranger was scarcely a boy, as Esther had definitely termed him, but Greenberg reasoned that her term was merely wish-fulfillment, and he jauntily ran up behind him.

He allowed a few minutes to pass, for the man to intro-

duce himself and let Esther and Rosie don their company
manners. Then, secure in the knowledge that there would
be no scene until the guest left, he entered.

He waded through a hostile atmosphere, urbanely shook
hands with Sammie Katz, who was a doctor—probably,
Greenberg thought shrewdly, in search of an office—and
excused himself.

In the bathroom he carefully read the directions for using
brushless shaving cream. He felt less confident when he
realized that he had to wash his face thoroughly with soap
and water, but without benefit of either, he spread the cream
on, patted it, and waited for his beard to soften. It did not,
as he discovered while shaving. He wiped his face dry. The
towel was sticky and black, with whiskers suspended in
paste, and, for that, he knew, there would be more hell to
pay. He shrugged resignedly. He would have to spend fifteen dollars for an electric razor after all; this foolishness
was costing him a fortune!

That they were waiting for him before beginning supper
was, he knew, only a gesture for the sake of company. Without changing her hard, brilliant smile, Esther whispered:
"Wait! I'll get you later—"

He smiled back, his tortured, slashed face creasing painfully. All that could be changed by his being enormously
pleasant to Rosie's young man. If he could slip Sammie a
few dollars—more expense, he groaned—to take Rosie out,
Esther would forgive everything.

He was too engaged in beaming and putting Sammie at
ease to think of what would happen after he ate caviar can-
apes. Under other circumstances Greenberg would have

been repulsed by Sammie's ultra-professional waxed mustache—an offensively small, pointed thing—and his commercial attitude toward poor Rosie; but Greenberg regarded him as a potential savior.

"You open an office yet, Doctor Katz?"

"Not yet. You know how things are. Anyhow, call me Sammie."

Greenberg recognized the gambit with satisfaction, since it seemed to please Esther so much. At one stroke Sammie had ingratiated himself and begun bargaining negotiations.

Without another word, Greenberg lifted his spoon to attack the soup. It would be easy to snare this eager doctor. A *doctor!* No wonder Esther and Rosie were so puffed with joy.

In the proper company way, he pushed his spoon away from him. The soup spilled onto the tablecloth.

"Not so hard, you dope," Esther hissed.

He drew the spoon toward him. The soup leaped off it like a live thing and splashed over him—turning, just before contact, to fall on the floor. He gulped and pushed the bowl away. This time the soup poured over the side of the plate and lay in a huge puddle on the table.

"I didn't want any soup anyhow," he said in a horrible attempt at levity. Lucky for him, he thought wildly, that Sammie was there to pacify Esther with his smooth college talk—not a bad fellow, Sammie, in spite of his mustache; he'd come in handy at times.

Greenberg lapsed into a paralysis of fear. He was thirsty after having eaten the caviar, which beats herring any time as a thirst raiser. But the knowledge that he could not touch water without having it recoil and perhaps spill, made his thirst a monumental craving. He attacked the problem cunningly.

The others were talking rapidly and rather hysterically. He waited until his courage was equal to his thirst; then he leaned over the table with a glass in his hand. "Sammie, do you mind—a little water, huh?"

Sammie poured from a pitcher while Esther watched for more of his tricks. It was to be expected, but still he was shocked when the water exploded out of the glass directly at Sammie's only suit.

"If you'll excuse me," Sammie said angrily, "I don't like to eat with lunatics."

And he left, though Esther cried and begged him to stay. Rosie was too stunned to move. But when the door closed, Greenberg raised his agonized eyes to watch his wife stalk murderously toward him.

Greenberg stood on the boardwalk outside his concession and glared blearily at the peaceful, blue, highly unpleasant ocean. He wondered what would happen if he started at the edge of the water and strode out. He could probably walk right to Europe on dry land.

It was early—much too early for business—and he was tired. Neither he nor Esther had slept; and it was practically certain that the neighbors hadn't either. But above all he was incredibly thirsty.

In a spirit of experimentation, he mixed a soda. Of course its high water content made it slop onto the floor. For breakfast he had surreptitiously tried fruit juice and coffee, without success.

With his tongue dry to the point of furriness, he sat

weakly on a boardwalk bench in front of his concession. It was Friday morning, which meant that the day was clear, with a promise of intense heat. Had it been Saturday, it naturally would have been raining.

"This year," he moaned, "I'll be wiped out. If I can't mix sodas, why should beer stay in a glass for me? I thought I could hire a boy for ten dollars a week to run the hot-dog griddle; I could make sodas, and Esther could draw beer. All I can do is make hot dogs. Esther can still draw beer; but twenty or maybe twenty-five a week I got to pay a soda-man. I won't even come out square—a fortune I'll lose!"

The situation really was desperate. Concessions depend on too many factors to be anything but capriciously profitable.

His throat was fiery and his soft brown eyes held a fierce glaze when the gas and electric were turned on, the beer pipes connected, the tank of carbon dioxide hitched to the pump, and the refrigerator started.

Gradually, the beach was filling with bathers. Greenberg writhed on his bench and envied them. They could swim and drink without having liquids draw away from them as if in horror. They were not thirsty—

And then he saw his first customers approach. His business experience was that morning customers buy only soft drinks. In a mad haste he put up the shutters and fled to the hotel.

"Esther!" he cried. "I got to tell you! I can't stand it—"

Threateningly, his wife held her broom like a baseball bat. "Go back to the concession, you crazy fool! Ain't you done enough already?"

He could not be hurt more than he had been. For once he did not cringe. "You got to help me, Esther."

"Why didn't you shave, you no-good bum? Is that any way—"

"That's what I got to tell you. Yesterday I got into an argument with a water gnome—"

"A *what?*" Esther looked at him suspiciously.

"A water gnome," he babbled in a rush of words. "A little man so high, with big ears that he swims with, and he makes it rain—"

"Herman!" she screamed. "Stop that nonsense. You're crazy!"

Greenberg pounded his forehead with his fist. "I *ain't* crazy. Look, Esther. Come with me into the kitchen."

She followed him readily enough, but her attitude made him feel more helpless and alone than ever. With her fists on her plump hips and her feet set wide, she cautiously watched him try to fill a glass of water.

"Don't you see?" he wailed. "It won't go in the glass. It spills all over. It runs away from me."

She was puzzled. "What happened to you?"

Brokenly, Greenberg told of his encounter with the water gnome, leaving out no single degrading detail. "And now I can't touch water," he ended. "I can't drink it. I can't make sodas. On top of it all, I got such a thirst, it's killing me."

Esther's reaction was instantaneous. She threw her arms around him, drew his head down to her shoulder, and patted him comfortingly as if he were a child. "Herman, my poor Herman!" she breathed tenderly. "What did we ever do to deserve such a curse?"

"What shall I do, Esther?" he cried helplessly.

She held him at arm's length. "You got to go to a doctor," she said firmly. "How long can you go without drinking? Without water you'll die. Maybe sometimes I am a little hard on you, but you know I love you—"

"I know, Mamma," he sighed. "But how can a doctor help me?"

"Am I a doctor that I should know? Go anyhow. What can you lose?"

He hesitated. "I need fifteen dollars for an electric razor," he said in a low, weak voice.

"So?" she replied. "If you got to, you got to. Go, darling. I'll take care of the concession."

Greenberg no longer felt deserted and alone. He walked almost confidently to a doctor's office. Manfully, he explained his symptoms. The doctor listened with professional sympathy, until Greenberg reached his description of the water gnome.

Then his eyes glittered and narrowed. "I know just the thing for you, Mr. Greenberg," he interrupted. "Sit there until I come back."

Greenberg sat quietly. He even permitted himself a surge of hope. But it seemed only a moment later that he was vaguely conscious of a siren screaming toward him; and then he was overwhelmed by the doctor and two interns who pounced on him and tried to squeeze him into a bag.

He resisted, of course. He was terrified enough to punch wildly. "What are you doing to me?" he shrieked. "Don't put that thing on me!"

"Easy now," the doctor soothed. "Everything will be all right."

It was on that humiliating scene that the policeman, required by law to accompany public ambulances, appeared. "What's up?" he asked.

"Don't stand there, you fathead," an intern shouted. "This man's crazy. Help us get him into this strait jacket."

But the policeman approached indecisively. "Take it easy, Mr. Greenberg. They ain't gonna hurt you while I'm here. What's it all about?"

"Mike!" Greenberg cried, and clung to his protector's sleeve. "They think I'm crazy—"

"Of course he's crazy," the doctor stated. "He came in here with a fantastic yarn about a water gnome putting a curse on him."

"What kind of a curse, Mr. Greenberg?" Mike asked cautiously.

"I got into an argument with the water gnome who makes it rain and takes care of the fish," Greenberg blurted. "I tore up his hat. Now he won't let water touch me. I can't drink, or anything—"

The doctor nodded. "There you are. Absolutely insane."

"Shut up." For a long moment Mike stared curiously at Greenberg. Then: "Did any of you scientists think of testing him? Here, Mr. Greenberg." He poured water into a paper cup and held it out.

Greenberg moved to take it. The water backed up against the cup's far lip; when he took it in his hand, the water shot out into the air.

"Crazy, is he?" Mike asked with heavy irony. "I guess you

don't know there's things like gnomes and elves. Come with me, Mr. Greenberg."

They went out together and walked toward the boardwalk. Greenberg told Mike the entire story and explained how, besides being so uncomfortable to him personally, it would ruin him financially.

"Well, doctors can't help you," Mike said at length. "What do they know about the Little Folk? And I can't say I blame you for sassing the gnome. You ain't Irish or you'd have spoke with more respect to him. Anyhow, you're thirsty. Can't you drink *anything?*"

"Not a thing," Greenberg said mournfully.

They entered the concession. A single glance told Greenberg that business was very quiet, but even that could not lower his feelings more than they already were. Esther clutched him as soon as she saw them.

"Well?" she asked anxiously.

Greenberg shrugged in despair. "Nothing. He thought I was crazy."

Mike stared at the bar. Memory seemed to struggle behind his reflective eyes. "Sure," he said after a long pause. "Did you try beer, Mr. Greenberg? When I was a boy my old mother told me all about elves and gnomes and the rest of the Little Folk. She knew them, all right. They don't touch alcohol, you know. Try drawing a glass of beer."

Greenberg trudged obediently behind the bar and held a glass under the spigot. Suddenly his despondent face brightened. Beer creamed into the glass—and stayed there! Mike and Esther grinned at each other as Greenberg threw back his head and furiously drank.

"Mike!" he crowed. "I'm saved. You got to drink with me!"

"Well—" Mike protested feebly.

By late afternoon, Esther had to close the concession and take her husband and Mike to the hotel.

The following day, being Saturday, brought a flood of rain. Greenberg nursed an imposing hangover that was constantly aggravated by his having to drink beer in order to satisfy his recurring thirst. He thought of forbidden icebags and alkaline drinks in an agony of longing.

"I can't stand it!" he groaned. "Beer for breakfast—phooey!"

"It's better than nothing," Esther said fatalistically.

"So help me, I don't know if it is. But, darling, you ain't mad at me on account of Sammie, are you?"

She smiled gently. "Poo! Talk dowry and he'll come back quick."

"That's what I thought. But what am I going to do about my curse?"

Cheerfully Mike furled an umbrella and strode in with a little old woman, whom he introduced as his mother. Greenberg enviously saw evidence of the effectiveness of icebags and alkaline drinks, for Mike had been just as high as he the day before.

"Mike told me about you and the gnome," the old lady said. "Now I know the Little Folk well, and I don't hold you to blame for insulting him, seeing you never met a gnome before. But I suppose you want to get rid of your curse. Are you repentant?"

Greenberg shuddered. "Beer for breakfast! Can you ask?"

"Well, just you go to this lake and give the gnome proof."

"What kind of proof?" Greenberg asked eagerly.

"Bring him sugar. The Little Folk love the stuff—"

Greenberg beamed. "Did you hear that, Esther? I'll get a barrel—"

"They love sugar, but they can't eat it," the old lady broke in. "It melts in water. You got to figure out a way so it won't. Then the little gentleman'll know you're repentant for real."

"A-ha!" Greenberg cried. "I knew there was a catch!"

There was a sympathetic silence while his agitated mind attacked the problem from all angles. Then the old lady said in awe: "The minute I saw your place I knew Mike had told the truth. I never seen a sight like it in my life—rain coming down, like the flood, everywhere else; but all around this place, in a big circle, it's dry as a bone!"

While Greenberg scarcely heard her, Mike nodded and Esther seemed peculiarly interested in the phenomenon. When he admitted defeat and came out of his reflective stupor, he was alone in the concession, with only a vague memory of Esther's saying she would not be back for several hours.

"What am I going to do?" he muttered. "Sugar that won't melt—" He drew a glass of beer and drank it thoughtfully. "Particular they got to be yet. Ain't it good enough if I bring simple syrup?—that's sweet."

He pottered about the place, looking for something to do. He could not polish the fountain or the bar, and the few frankfurters broiling on the griddle probably would go to

waste. The floor had already been swept. So he sat uneasily
and worried his problem.

"Monday, no matter what," he resolved, "I'll go to the
lake. It don't pay to go tomorrow. I'll only catch a cold because it'll rain."

At last Esther returned, smiling in a strange way. She
was extremely gentle, tender and thoughtful; and for that
he was appreciative. But that night and all day Sunday he
understood the reason for her happiness.

She had spread word that, while it rained in every other
place all over town, their concession was miraculously
dry. So, besides a headache that made his body throb in
rhythm to its vast pulse, Greenberg had to work like six
men satisfying the crowd who mobbed the place to see the
miracle and enjoy the dry warmth.

How much they took in will never be known. Greenberg
made it a practice not to discuss such personal matters. But
it is quite definite that not even in 1929 had he done so well
over a single weekend.

Very early Monday morning he was dressing quietly, not
to disturb his wife. Esther, however, raised herself on her
elbow and looked at him doubtfully.

"Herman," she called softly, "do you really have to go?"

He turned, puzzled. "What do you mean—do I have
to go?"

"Well—" She hesitated. Then: "Couldn't you wait until
the end of the season, Herman, darling?"

He staggered back a step, his face working in horror.
"What kind of an idea is that for my own wife to have?" he
croaked. "Beer I have to drink instead of water. How can I

stand it? Do you think I *like* beer? I can't wash myself. Already people don't like to stand near me; and how will they act at the end of the season? I go around looking like a bum because my beard is too tough for an electric razor, and I'm all the time drunk—the first Greenberg to be a drunkard. I want to be respected—"

"I know, Herman, darling," she sighed. "But I thought for the sake of our Rosie— Such a business we've never done like we did this weekend. If it rains every Saturday and Sunday, but not on our concession, we'll make a *fortune!*"

"Esther!" Herman cried, shocked. "Doesn't my health mean anything?"

"Of course, darling. Only I thought maybe you could stand it for—"

He snatched his hat, tie and jacket, and slammed the door. Outside, though, he stood indeterminedly. He could hear his wife crying, and he realized that, if he succeeded in getting the gnome to remove the curse, he would forfeit an opportunity to make a great deal of money.

He finished dressing more slowly. Esther was right, to a certain extent. If he could tolerate his waterless condition—

"No!" he gritted decisively. "Already my friends avoid me. It isn't right that a respectable man like me should always be drunk and not take a bath. So we'll make less money. Money isn't everything—"

And with great determination he went to the lake.

But that evening, before going home, Mike walked out of his way to stop in at the concession. He found Greenberg sitting on a chair, his head in his hands, and his body rocking slowly in anguish.

"What is it, Mr. Greenberg?" he asked gently.

Greenberg looked up. His eyes were dazed. "Oh, you, Mike," he said blankly. Then his gaze cleared, grew more intelligent, and he stood up and led Mike to the bar. Silently, they drank beer. "I went to the lake today," he said hollowly. "I walked all around it, hollering like mad. The gnome didn't stick his head out of the water once."

"I know." Mike nodded sadly. "They're busy all the time."

Greenberg spread his hands imploringly. "So what can I do? I can't write him a letter or send him a telegram; he ain't got a door to knock on or a bell for me to ring. How do I get him to come up and talk?"

His shoulders sagged. "Here, Mike. Have a cigar. You been a real good friend, but I guess we're licked."

They stood in an awkward silence. Finally Mike blurted: "Real hot, today. A regular scorcher."

"Yeah. Esther says business was pretty good, if it keeps up."

Mike fumbled at the cellophane wrapper. Greenberg said: "Anyhow, suppose I did talk to the gnome. What about the sugar?"

The silence dragged itself out, became tense and uncomfortable. Mike was distinctly embarrassed. His brusque nature was not adapted for comforting discouraged friends. With immense concentration he rolled the cigar between his fingers and listened for a rustle.

"Day like this's hell on cigars," he mumbled, for the sake of conversation. "Dries them like nobody's business. This one ain't, though."

"Yeah," Greenberg said abstractedly. "Cellophane keeps them—"

They looked suddenly at each other, their faces clean of expression.

"Holy smoke!" Mike yelled.

"Cellophane on sugar!" Greenberg choked out.

"Yeah," Mike whispered in awe. "I'll switch my day off with Joe, and I'll go to the lake with you tomorrow. I'll call for you early."

Greenberg pressed his hand, too strangled by emotion for speech. When Esther came to relieve him, he left her at the concession with only the inexperienced griddle boy to assist her, while he searched the village for cubes of sugar wrapped in cellophane.

The sun had scarcely risen when Mike reached the hotel, but Greenberg had long been dressed and stood on the porch waiting impatiently. Mike was genuinely anxious for his friend. Greenberg staggered along toward the station, his eyes almost crossed with the pain of a terrific hangover.

They stopped at a cafeteria for breakfast. Mike ordered orange juice, bacon and eggs, and coffee half-and-half. When he heard the order, Greenberg had to gag down a lump in his throat.

"What'll you have?" the counterman asked.

Greenberg flushed. "Beer," he said hoarsely.

"You kidding me?" Greenberg shook his head, unable to speak. "Want anything with it? Cereal, pie, toast—"

"Just beer." And he forced himself to swallow it. "So help me," he hissed at Mike, "another beer for breakfast will kill me!"

"I know how it is," Mike said around a mouthful of food.

On the train they attempted to make plans. But they were faced by a phenomenon that neither had encountered before, and so they got nowhere. They walked glumly to the lake, fully aware that they would have to employ the empirical method of discarding tactics that did not work.

"How about a boat?" Mike suggested.

"It won't stay in the water with me in it. And you can't row it."

"Well, what'll we do then?"

Greenberg bit his lip and stared at the beautiful blue lake. There the gnome lived, so near to them. "Go through the woods along the shore, and holler like hell. I'll go the opposite way. We'll pass each other and meet at the boathouse. If the gnome comes up, yell for me."

"O.K.," Mike said, not very confidently.

The lake was quite large and they walked slowly around it, pausing often to get the proper stance for particularly emphatic shouts. But two hours later, when they stood opposite each other with the full diameter of the lake between them, Greenberg heard Mike's hoarse voice: "Hey, gnome!"

"Hey, gnome!" Greenberg yelled. "Come on up!"

An hour later they crossed paths. They were tired, discouraged, and their throats burned; and only fishermen disturbed the lake's surface.

"The hell with this," Mike said. "It ain't doing any good. Let's go back to the boathouse."

"What'll we do?" Greenberg rasped. "I can't give up!"

They trudged back around the lake, shouting half-heartedly. At the boathouse, Greenberg had to admit that he was beaten. The boathouse owner marched threateningly toward them.

"Why don't you maniacs get away from here?" he barked.

"What's the idea of hollering and scaring away the fish? The guys are sore—"

"We're not going to holler any more," Greenberg said. "It's no use."

When they bought beer and Mike, on an impulse, hired a boat, the owner cooled off with amazing rapidity, and went off to unpack bait.

"What did you get a boat for?" Greenberg asked. "I can't ride in it."

"You're not going to. You're gonna walk."

"Around the lake again?" Greenberg cried.

"Nope. Look, Mr. Greenberg. Maybe the gnome can't hear us through all that water. Gnomes ain't hardhearted. If he heard us and thought you were sorry, he'd take the curse off you in a jiffy."

"Maybe." Greenberg was not convinced. "So where do I come in?"

"The way I figure it, some way or other you push water away, but the water pushes you away just as hard. Anyhow, I hope so. If it does, you can walk on the lake." As he spoke, Mike had been lifting large stones and dumping them on the bottom of the boat. "Give me a hand with these."

Any activity, however useless, was better than none, Greenberg felt. He helped Mike fill the boat until just the gunwhales were above water. Then Mike got in and shoved off.

"Come on," Mike said. "Try to walk on the water."

Greenberg hesitated. "Suppose I can't?"

"Nothing'll happen to you. You can't get wet, so you won't drown."

The logic of Mike's statement reassured Greenberg. He

stepped out boldly. He experienced a peculiar sense of accomplishment when the water hastily retreated under his feet into pressure bowls, and an unseen, powerful force buoyed him upright across the lake's surface. Though his footing was not too secure, with care he was able to walk quite swiftly.

"Now what?" he asked, almost happily.

Mike had kept pace with him in the boat. He shipped his oars and passed Greenberg a rock. "We'll drop them all over the lake—make it damned noisy down there and upset the place. That'll get him up."

They were more hopeful now, and their comments, "Here's one that'll wake him," and "I'll hit him right on the noodle with this one," served to cheer them still further. And less than half the rocks had been dropped when Greenberg halted, a boulder in his hands. Something inside him wrapped itself tightly around his heart and his jaw dropped.

Mike followed his awed, joyful gaze. To himself Mike had to admit that the gnome, propelling himself through the water with his ears, arms folded in tremendous dignity, was a funny sight.

"Must you drop rocks and disturb us at our work?" the gnome asked.

Greenberg gulped. "I'm sorry, Mr. Gnome," he said nervously, "I couldn't get you to come up by yelling."

The gnome looked at him. "Oh. You are the mortal who was disciplined. Why did you return?"

"To tell you that I'm sorry, and I won't insult you again."

"Have you proof of your sincerity?" the gnome asked quietly.

Greenberg fished furiously in his pocket and brought out

a handful of sugar wrapped in cellophane, which he trem-
blingly handed to the gnome.

"Ah, very clever, indeed," the little man said, unwrapping
a cube and popping it eagerly into his mouth. "Long time
since I've had some."

A moment later Greenberg spluttered and floundered
under the surface. Even if Mike had not caught his jacket
and helped him up, he could almost have enjoyed the sensation of being able to drown.

In Heinlein's "They" we met a theme which has fueled some of the most powerful writing ever done in imaginative fiction. Here it is again, in a different and more evocative, perhaps more disturbing, form. Who are you, really—and how do you know you are?

Peter Phillips

C/O
MR. MAKEPEACE

Regard London suburbanites. Then abandon the attempt at crystalline classification. The suburbanite tag is the only thing they have in common.

Some commute. Others tend their gardens. The brick boxes of city clerks sidle up close to the fifteen-room mansions of stockbrokers. The party wall of a semi-detached villa is a barrier between universes; in this half lives a sweetly respectable retired grocer; in the other, a still-active second-storey man with a fat and ailing wife and a nymphomaniac daughter.

Sometimes there's a community sense. But more often, neighbors stay strangers throughout their lives.

For instance, no one knew 50-year-old Tristram Makepeace. Not even himself.

British reserve can be a damnably frightening thing.

One morning, in the long, winding, tree-lined avenue in the so-suburban suburb where he lived—

"Hey!"

The postman turned at the gate. Tristram Makepeace hurried down the path of his neat, bush-enclosed front garden, leaving the door of his villa open.

"Not here," he said, and held out an envelope.

The postman took it, read the typewritten address.

E. Grabcheek, Esq.,
c/o Tristram Makepeace,
36, Acacia Avenue.

The postman, blank-faced, looked at the thin, tall, hollow-cheeked bachelor. "That's you, sir, isn't it? And it's your address."

Makepeace drew his dressing gown closer against the chill morning air. His voice was high, with limited range of inflection. "But I don't know anyone named Grabcheek. There's certainly no one staying with me. It's lucky I was up in time for the delivery this morning. I'm not, as a rule, you know."

But the postman returned the letter firmly. "Can't take it back. Sorry. They'd only send it out with the next round. Sure you don't know anyone called Grabcheek?"

"Of course I'm sure. I can't accept delivery."

The postman hesitated, made a slow admission. "It's none of my business," he said. "I usually just look at the address. But knowing you live alone—well, it caught my eye. You *did* accept delivery, you know, just the other day. The name stuck in my mind: Grabcheek. And there was another before that."

Makepeace blinked pale eyes, disturbed. "But I didn't—I haven't seen anything like this before." He fluttered the envelope.

"Well, I shoved 'em through your door. Right address as far as I'm concerned. Now I've got to get on; I'm behind time already."

"But this is ridiculous. Look here, my man—"

The postman, determinedly preoccupied, duty-bound, snapped the gate shut behind him. "Look under the mat," he said, without glancing up from the sheaf of letters in his hand; and he walked on, leaving ex-Captain Makepeace very much alone in the world.

Makepeace looked under the coir mat near his front door as he went back in. Dust. Blasted dust everywhere in this place. But no letters. Anyway, falling from the letterbox in the door, they couldn't have slid under the mat. The postman was a fool, or mistaken.

But—Grabcheek was not the sort of name one would forget.

He examined the envelope. A local postmark. He held it up to the light through the glass-panelled door. Nothing showed through. Envelope too thick.

Not for a moment did it occur to Tristram Makepeace to open it. He just wasn't the sort of man to open another person's letters. Which should indicate what sort of man he was.

After his inadequate breakfast of tea and toast, he re-enclosed the letter in a larger envelope and addressed it to the Post Office in High Street, with a terse note typewritten on his old portable: "No one of that name here . . . T. Makepeace."

Then he made a few ineffectual flicks at dust. Sometimes he wished he could borrow the vacuum cleaner from the woman next door; a little like tanks they were, the way they mopped up the dusty opposition. But the neighbor just looked at him with a polite "good morning." And he daren't ask her. He went to cash his pension cheque, and re-posted the double letter on the way.

He mustn't worry about the letter. That was a sure way

to bring back his old trouble. Worrying. And about nothing at all.

Mustn't worry. He had his house, his pension, his garden, his books, his acquaintances at the local public house.

He went in there, on his way home, spent his pension more liberally than usual.

He told the regulars about his mystery.

"Should have opened the bloody thing," grunted the landlord, irritated with honesty that could perpetuate such a mystery.

"Fancy telling us," said a straight-gin widow, also annoyed. "Now we might never know."

Makepeace looked round the bar. "No one here called Grabcheek, I suppose?"

A shaking of heads.

When he got home that afternoon, a little drunk, there had been a second postal delivery.

> E. Grabcheek, Esq.,
> c/o Tristram Makepeace,
> 36, Acacia Avenue.

He thrust the letter into the pocket of his old tweed jacket, went upstairs to sleep on the bed he had forgotten to tidy that morning.

He awoke with a dry mouth in the early evening, memories of the day blurred. He put his hand in his jacket pocket. There was no letter. He shrugged.

Mind overlapping itself, Tristram: don't you remember—you posted it back to the post office. . . . Or was that another one? Doesn't matter. Don't worry.

Two days later, Tristram Makepeace, after a night disturbed by dreams of flowers floating over a desert, was up again in time to hear the postman's early double knock.

Two letters were lying on the dusty coir mat. One was for:

> E. Grabcheek, Esq.,
> c/o Tristram Makepeace,
> 36, Acacia Avenue.

The other, officially franked, was for him. It contained the earlier letter to Grabcheek and a note from the local post office: ". . . must inform you that this letter was properly delivered, and we have no authority. . . ."

Makepeace did not open either of the Grabcheek letters he held in his shaky hands in that dusty hallway.

Don't blame or praise him. He was the sum of what others had made him, and deep, deep, was his dead father saying: *It's just not done to open other people's letters, old man.*

He sent both letters, unopened, to the Postmaster General of Great Britain and Northern Ireland.

He got them back from the PMG's secretary's secretary, unopened, with red-tape regrets, on a strange and sunny morning a week later. A covering note of eyebrow-raised politeness suggested that, as the occupier of the villa, he might have a *right* to open them.

Very well.

He would. Blast his father.

Oh no no no he didn't mean that, truly he didn't mean that, what a silly thing to say anyway, and he hadn't said it, really, it was something outside him, something he wasn't

responsible for, so touch the wall three times and every-
thing will be all right. Don't worry. Mustn't worry.

Makepeace flung one of the Grabcheek letters on the
small table in the hallway. Dust fluffed up and made a sun-
beam visible.

He went into his dining room with the other letter and
sat down over the remains of his breakfast.

It must be all right to open it. All he had to do was read
the sender's address, then post it back "NOT KNOWN."

He opened it. The paper inside was blank.

Makepeace remembered some of his army language. He
swore for thirty seconds in his flat, high voice, then ripped
envelope and blank sheet into fragments.

"Silly bloody hoax," he said finally, and felt relieved.

He went out into the hall to do the same with the other
letter. It had disappeared from the table.

Then Mr. Makepeace, very empty, with time at a dead
stop in his blank, cold mind, fell to his knees and patted at
the dusty carpet. He breathed dust.

He got up. "It was there," he announced. "It was there, I
know. I threw it there, and I saw it lying there."

He thumb-and-fingered his twitching eyes and touched
the wall three times.

Dear father, I love you. Mustn't worry.

Of course he hadn't thrown the letter there. He'd taken
it into the dining room with the other one, and torn both
of them up into tiny scraps, and put them on the big wil-
low-pattern plate.

He went back into the dining room, not breathing very
deeply.

There was nothing on the plate, or on the table. No single fragment of paper.

The house was very still.

Of course, the postman hadn't called that morning at all. That was it. The whole thing was a damnable half-dream, one of those partly-controllable dreams, and he always felt sleepy in the mornings nowadays.

But the tingling feel of paper being torn. . . . He held himself stiff for a moment, refusing to think, forcing his mind to rare silence. Then, methodically, unhurried, he looked under the dining room table. He looked at the shut windows, fronting on Acacia Avenue. He searched the house, in cupboards, under beds, upstairs, downstairs.

In the coal cellar, he found himself idly turning over pieces of bad-quality coal, watching smooth black shiny surfaces reflect light from the tiny window. He had forgotten what he was searching for.

Half-automatically, army training having been superimposed on a crabbed and tidy childhood, he made his bed—he had forgotten to do it one day last week, and it had nagged his mind terribly—and went to the public house and drank a good deal of whisky. He looked out of the bar window, and talked to nobody.

In his mind there was—

Clum, clum, nick-nock, NO . . . hibbledy-hobbledy, hock, Christ on a thorn tree, NO; take a pair of sparkling eyes and see that tree. MY FATHER DEATH. Forgive me who's listening. I'm not responsible for whoever puts things like that in my mind, clum, clum, bibbledy-bo, the bastard inflicting this sort of thing on me. . . . No, God, I didn't say that, there's a cold clean sweet chopper coming for my head, this way the Rhine, that way home. . . . Rune, rune, ruin the rune, if I could master the compulsion the chopper would come quicker they say, or would say if they knew anything, so let it carry on. . . . I won't think my hands aren't dirty, I slapped him with my right hand when he was drunk because he hit my mother, but I apologized and explained. . . . STOP THINKING. . . . Or think of anything, even the barmaid's flabby breasts. . . . Mother. . . . NO. . . . the ashtray. . . . hard.

The glass ashtray on the table in front of Mr. Makepeace slithered over the beer-wet surface and splintered on the composition floor. He felt a little better, treated the publican to a drink, and went home down the tree-lined avenue to his villa and a lunch of sausages and worm-eaten spinach from his neglected garden.

After lunch, he took out his wallet to find the covering letter from the Postmaster General's secretary's secretary. He found nothing but the remainder of his pension, in crumpled notes.

He addressed himself to the wall. "I am not going mad," he said, without emphasis. "I am not going mad."

That was one of the things he had told himself when an unexpected German shell, ravishing the peaceful sky, had burst near him.

When he felt pain in his spine and head, undeserved pain, unfair pain, he had struggled to his feet near the demolished signal post. He had seen his father's big, lined, hard face in the sky, and as he fell back again to the tumbled brown earth, he said, without moving paralyzed lips:

"That was a dirty trick, Daddy. You shouldn't have done that. You shouldn't have hit my mother, the sky. . . . But I am not going mad. I am not going mad."

In the field hospital, sitting up as a nurse washed him, he had clearly seen the back of his own neck. And that night, he had perched on the end of his own bed and watched himself sleeping.

Long lemon-washed corridors, with inset black doors, had presaged his final discharge from His Majesty's Service. Beyond one certain black door a neurologist—or a psychiatrist—or at least a mechanistic psychologist—had told him: "We shall recommend you for a forty-per-cent pension. If you have any more of these subjective—um—experiences in between your half-yearly examinations, just report to the Ministry of Pensions."

A thousand forms weaving through blue-shot air: forms AH 5647/45 (Officer, RAC. Med. Inf., 34), (Din. 01/16 7896), Hos. X. (F.P./2333)—S.O.—

And now—

It was all subjective, of course. The Grabcheek letters. The Grabcheek Letters, giving them undeserved caps. Like a book he'd read once. . . . What was it? . . . It didn't matter. . . . When his head was clear again he'd reread his whole shelf of belles-lettres. . . . Lamb. Whose Lamb led to what unexplained slaughter?

Sometime, said Mr. Makepeace to himself, with what little was left of his conscious mind, I must distemper the walls of this room again.

Meantime, he must obey orders.

Write to the Ministry. Ask for an examination. Write now.

Or wait until tomorrow, when he could check with the postman whether he had called that morning.

Now it was late afternoon, with an old, yellow sun putting cheap gilt on the roofs of the houses over the way. Now it was too late to write, anyway, for the last post had gone. Tomorrow would do. Tomorrow would always do.

Now was the time to walk down to the local public house and tell some quite untrue tales of his soldiering days, after taking the edge off his reserve with whisky.

"'E's quite a character when 'e's 'ad one or two. . . . Lives all alone in Acacia Avenue. . . . Why don't 'e marry? Ask 'im. . . . Always good for a gin, though. . . . Queer old bird."

Mr. Makepeace walked into the hallway and examined himself in the mirror.

Old? At 50?

Yes, and tired.

He went to bed.

He waited at his dining room bay window the next morning, watching the slow progress of the postman who seemed to be calling at almost every house on his side of the avenue.

He waited until the postman was about to open his front garden gate, then hurried to meet him.

> E. Grabcheek, Esq.,
> c/o Tristram Makepeace,
> 36, Acacia Avenue.

Makepeace was aware of the cold morning air, the gravel underfoot, a blackbird singing from the laurel bushes, milk bottles clinking together somewhere nearby, the postman's stupid unshaven face; and, faintly, from a neighboring house, "This is the B.B.C. Home Service. Here is the eight o'clock news. . . ."

"Found out who he is yet?" asked the postman.

"No."

Tristram Makepeace turned back along the path towards his house. It was waiting for him. The door into the ever-dusty hallway was open. It was the mouth of the house, and it was open.

The eyes of the house, asymmetrical windows, were blazing, yellow and hungry in the early sun.

He wanted to run after the postman and talk with him; or go up the road to the milkman and ask him about his wife and children, talking and talking to reassert this life and his living of it.

But they would think he was mad; and he was not mad. The cold began to strike through his thin slippers and dressing gown, so he walked slowly back up the gravel pathway into the mouth of the house, and closed the door behind him.

He opened the envelope, took out the blank sheet, tore it through. The equal halves fluttered to the floor. He tried to keep his brain as blank as the sheet of paper. It would be nice, came the sudden thought, if he could take his brain out and wash it blank and white and clean under clear running water.

A dark, itching foulness compounded of a million uninvited pictures was trying to force its way into his mind . . . strike your god, your father, see him stand surprised with the red marks of your fingers on his cheek . . . and your lovely virgin mother. . . .

"NO!"

He shouted the negation, forced the pictures back, and stood trembling with the effort.

Three times three on this wall, three times three on that wall. . . . Keep it down, hard, and if you can't be blank, think blind. . . . If that barrier goes, I'm done for. . . . I need help.

Mr. Makepeace dressed, and sat down at his old typewriter to compose a sweetly pedantic letter to the Ministry of Pensions, asking for an interview by a psychiatrist.

He wrote, in part: "I cannot doubt the objective reality of these foolish hoax letters, since the postman would confirm that I have received them; but I fear that their subsequent apparent disappearance may be the result of short phases of amnesia, attended by false memories, in which I secretly destroy them. . . . Please treat this matter as urgent."

" 'Subsequent apparent disappearance,' " murmured a Ministry clerk. "Oh Gawd." He stamped the letter WRONG DEPARTMENT. PASSED TO MINISTRY OF HEALTH, and placed it in a tray for routine collection by interdepartmental messenger the next day.

On the second day of waiting, Mr. Makepeace's head was numb with the effort of not thinking.

His letter was routed through the Ministry of Health, marked FOR ATTENTION MEDICAL BOARD, DISTRICT E.

On the fourth day of waiting, as Mr. Makepeace sat head-in-hands at his breakfast table, the morning newspaper, which he had not bothered to pick up from the mat inside the front door, dropped through the ceiling, and spilt a cup of cold tea in front of him. He laughed.

Now he dared not leave his dusty house, for that would be running away. And he might meet a chance acquaintance who would pity him.

He looked over his shoulder and laughed again, a curious little high-pitched giggle. There were tears in his eyes.

The Secretary of the Medical Board, District E, on Form EOH/563, wrote to an Army Medical Board, asking for the case-history papers relating to ex-Captain Tristram Makepeace.

On the fifth day of waiting, thin, proud, foolish Mr. Makepeace, who had no intimate friends, no near relations, no anchor in slipping reality, and no imagination, spent the day walking round inside his house and addressing each face of each inner wall, three times each time, with a new compulsive rune designed to cleanse the inner walls of his brain of an accretion of dust.

On the morning of the seventh day, the woman next door hastily phoned for an ambulance.

Mr. Makepeace, pale eyes quite blank in his gaunt face, was leaning from his bedroom window, and screaming.

She made out a few words: "The barrier's down . . . I can't stand it."

"He must have been fighting that Oedipus-complex cycle for years," said the Superintendent thoughtfully. "Then—*phut* —sheer pressure plunges him into psychosis." He looked again at the encephalograph. "A classical schizophrenic overnight."

"Be damned," said his young assistant. "No ordinary

schizo—save the mark—ever exhibits such a clear-cut, contrasting duality."

"Which is he this morning?" asked the Superintendent.

"Grabcheek, writing himself another letter care of Tristram Makepeace. The handwriting is quite distinctive. Incidentally, police checked on those Grabcheek envelopes we found in his pockets. They were definitely typed on his machine."

"But no actual letters were found—only blank sheets. So what is he writing now?"

The young assistant stared out of the office window. "'Your father sends you his best wishes, and hopes he will meet you soon,'" he quoted.

"Poor devil," said the Superintendent. "At least he can't post them to himself now."

The assistant drew a sealed envelope from his pocket. "This was in the mail this morning. We had to pay excess postage because it wasn't stamped."

> E. Grabcheek, Esq.,
> c/o Tristram Makepeace,
> Seaton Mental Hospital
> Essex.

The Superintendent jerked upright in his chair. "But how in the name of heaven. . . . He's been isolated here for the past week!"

"A self-haunted man isn't bound by the three-dimensional limitations of his main personality. Read a few case-histories of poltergeist phenomena and you'll see what I mean. The poltergeist is not a ghost. It is a bundle of projected repressions.' That's a quote from a book you refused to read. Remember?"

"Nonsense," muttered the Superintendent. "A dissociated personality cannot have a separate objective existence!"

"According to that book it can," the other persisted. "You might give it a try: *Haunted People,* by Hereward Carrington and Nandor Fodor. Fodor even encountered such dissociations in his psychiatric practice."

"No . . . *No!*" the Superintendent said sharply. "Someone smuggled that letter out for him and posted it."

"Without a stamp?" The assistant grinned. The grin faded.

"It's a damnable theory," he admitted. "The other personality is almost invariably evil. In Tibet, adepts deliberately purge their minds of what we would call neurotic symbolism by projecting *thanai*—thoughts which coalesce into evil spirits, which are then dissipated. Or not."

"And thus," said the Superintendent, "the Abominable Snowman?" He laughed.

At an empty house in a so-suburban suburb that morning, the postman delivered a final letter. It fluttered to the doormat. It was addressed—without the concession of a c/o now —to:

Ezreel Grabcheek, Esq.,
36, Acacia Avenue.

As the footsteps of the preoccupied, duty-bound postman died away, the letter zig-zagged upwards from the mat, poised in mid-air.

Something laughed.

Here is the first of two stories on the Frankenstein theme; the other will be along a little later and is serious; this one is not.

This story is a marvel of compactness and ease; I do not see how it could be improved by so much as a word.

Avram Davidson

THE GOLEM

The gray-faced person came along the street where old Mr. and Mrs. Gumbeiner lived. It was afternoon, it was autumn, the sun was warm and soothing to their ancient bones. Anyone who attended the movies in the twenties or the early thirties has seen that street a thousand times. Past these bungalows with their half-double roofs Edmund Lowe walked arm-in-arm with Leatrice Joy and Harold Lloyd was chased by Chinamen waving hatchets. Under these squamous palm trees Laurel kicked Hardy and Woolsey beat Wheeler upon the head with a codfish. Across these pocket-handkerchief-sized lawns the juveniles of the Our Gang Comedies pursued one another and were pursued by angry fat men in golf knickers. On this same street—or perhaps on some other one of five hundred streets exactly like it.

Mrs. Gumbeiner indicated the gray-faced person to her husband.

"You think maybe he's got something the matter?" she asked. "He walks kind of funny, to me."

"Walks like a *golem*," Mr. Gumbeiner said indifferently.

The old woman was nettled.

"Oh, I don't know," she said. "*I* think he walks like your cousin Mendel."

The old man pursed his mouth angrily and chewed on his pipestem. The gray-faced person turned up the concrete

path, walked up the steps to the porch, sat down in a chair.
Old Mr. Gumbeiner ignored him. His wife stared at the
stranger.

"Man comes in without a hello, goodby, or howareyou,
sits himself down and right away he's at home. . . . The
chair is comfortable?" she asked. "Would you like maybe
a glass tea?"

She turned to her husband.

"Say something, Gumbeiner!" she demanded. "What are
you, made of wood?"

The old man smiled a slow, wicked, triumphant smile.

"Why should *I* say anything?" he asked the air. "Who
am I? Nothing, that's who."

The stranger spoke. His voice was harsh and monotonous.

"When you learn who—or, rather, what—I am, the flesh
will melt from your bones in terror." He bared porcelain
teeth.

"Never mind about my bones!" the old woman cried.
"You've got a lot of nerve talking about my bones!"

"You will quake with fear," said the stranger. Old Mrs.
Gumbeiner said that she hoped he would live so long. She
turned to her husband once again.

"Gumbeiner, when are you going to mow the lawn?"

"All mankind—" the stranger began.

"*Shah!* I'm talking to my husband. . . . He talks *eppis*
kind of funny, Gumbeiner, no?"

"Probably a foreigner," Mr. Gumbeiner said, compla-
cently.

"You think so?" Mrs. Gumbeiner glanced fleetingly at
the stranger. "He's got a very bad color in his face, *nebbich*,
I suppose he came to California for his health."

"Disease, pain, sorrow, love, grief—all are nought to—"
Mr. Gumbeiner cut in on the stranger's statement.

"Gall bladder," the old man said. "Guinzburg down at
the *shule* looked exactly the same before his operation.
Two professors they had in for him, and a private nurse
day and night."

"I am not a human being!" the stranger said loudly.

"Three thousand seven hundred fifty dollars it cost his
son, Guinzburg told me. 'For you, Poppa, nothing is too
expensive—only get well,' the son told him."

"I am not a human being!"

"Ai, is that a son for you!" the old woman said, rocking
her head. "A heart of gold, pure gold." She looked at the
stranger. "All right, all right, I heard you the first time.
Gumbeiner! I asked you a question. When are you going
to cut the lawn?"

"On Wednesday, *odder* maybe Thursday, comes the Japaneser to the neighborhood. To cut lawns is *his* profession.
My profession is to be a glazier—retired."

"Between me and all mankind is an inevitable hatred,"
the stranger said. "When I tell you what I am, the flesh will
melt—"

"You said, you said already," Mr. Gumbeiner interrupted.

"In Chicago where the winters were as cold and bitter as
the Czar of Russia's heart," the old woman intoned, "you had
strength to carry the frames with the glass together day in
and day out. But in California with the golden sun to mow
the lawn when your wife asks, for this you have no strength.
Do I call in the Japaneser to cook for you supper?"

"Thirty years Professor Allardyce spent perfecting his
theories. Electronics, neuronics—"

"Listen, how educated he talks," Mr. Gumbeiner said, admiringly. "Maybe he goes to the University here?"

"If he goes to the University, maybe he knows Bud?" his wife suggested.

"Probably they're in the same class and he came to see him about the homework, no?"

"Certainly he must be in the same class. How many classes are there? Five *in ganzen:* Bud showed me on his program card." She counted off on her fingers. "Television Appreciation and Criticism, Small Boat Building, Social Adjustment, The American Dance. . . . The American Dance—*nu,* Gumbeiner—"

"Contemporary Ceramics," her husband said, relishing the syllables. "A fine boy, Bud. A pleasure to have him for a boardner."

"After thirty years spent in these studies," the stranger, who had continued to speak unnoticed, went on, "he turned from the theoretical to the pragmatic. In ten years' time he had made the most titanic discovery in history: he made mankind, *all* mankind, superfluous; he made *me.*"

"What did Tillie write in her last letter?" asked the old man.

The old woman shrugged.

"What should she write? The same thing. Sidney was home from the Army, Naomi has a new boy friend—"

"He made ME!"

"Listen, Mr. Whatever-your-name-is," the old woman said, "maybe where you came from is different, but in *this* country you don't interrupt people the while they're talking. . . . Hey. Listen—what do you mean, he *made* you? What kind of talk is that?"

The stranger bared all his teeth again, exposing the too-pink gums.

"In his library, to which I had a more complete access after his sudden and as yet undiscovered death from entirely natural causes, I found a complete collection of stories about androids, from Shelley's *Frankenstein* through Čapek's *R.U.R.* to Asimov's—"

"Frankenstein?" said the old man, with interest. "There used to be a Frankenstein who had the soda-*wasser* place on Halstead Street—a Litvack, *nebbich*."

"What are you talking?" Mrs. Gumbeiner demanded. "His name was Franken*thal*, and it wasn't on Halstead, it was on Roosevelt."

"—clearly shown that all mankind has an instinctive antipathy towards androids and there will be an inevitable struggle between them—"

"Of course, of course!" Old Mr. Gumbeiner clicked his teeth against his pipe. "I am always wrong, you are always right. How could you stand to be married to such a stupid person all this time?"

"I don't know," the old woman said. "Sometimes I wonder, myself. I think it must be his good looks." She began to laugh. Old Mr. Gumbeiner blinked, then began to smile, then took his wife's hand.

"Foolish old woman," the stranger said. "Why do you laugh? Do you not know I have come to destroy you?"

"What?" old Mr. Gumbeiner shouted. "Close your mouth, you!" He darted from his chair and struck the stranger with the flat of his hand. The stranger's head struck against the porch pillar and bounced back.

"When you talk to my wife, talk respectable, you hear?"

Old Mrs. Gumbeiner, cheeks very pink, pushed her husband back to his chair. Then she leaned forward and examined the stranger's head. She clicked her tongue as she pulled aside a flap of gray, skinlike material.

"Gumbeiner, look! He's all springs and wires inside!"

"I *told* you he was a *golem*, but no, you wouldn't listen," the old man said.

"You said he *walked* like a *golem*."

"How could he walk like a *golem* unless he *was* one?"

"All right, all right. . . . You broke him, so now fix him."

"My grandfather, his light shines from Paradise, told me that when MoHaRaL—Moreynu Ha-Rav Löw—his memory for a blessing, made the *golem* in Prague, three hundred? four hundred years ago? he wrote on his forehead the Holy Name."

Smiling reminiscently, the old woman continued, "And the *golem* cut the rabbi's wood and brought his water and guarded the ghetto."

"And one time only he disobeyed the Rabbi Löw, and Rabbi Löw erased the *Shem Ha-Mephorash* from the *golem's* forehead and the *golem* fell down like a dead one. And they put him up in the attic of the *shule* and he's still there today if the Communisten haven't sent him to Moscow. . . . This is not just a story," he said.

"*Avadda* not!" said the old woman.

"I myself have seen both the *shule and* the rabbi's grave," her husband said, conclusively.

"But I think this must be a different kind of *golem*, Gumbeiner. See, on his forehead; nothing written."

"What's the matter, there's a law I can't write something

there? Where is that lump clay Bud brought us from his class?"

The old man washed his hands, adjusted his little black skullcap, and slowly and carefully wrote four Hebrew letters on the gray forehead.

"Ezra the Scribe himself couldn't do better," the old woman said, admiringly. "Nothing happens," she observed, looking at the lifeless figure sprawled in the chair.

"Well, after all, am I Rabbi Löw?" her husband asked, deprecatingly. "No," he answered. He leaned over and examined the exposed mechanism. "This spring goes here . . . this wire comes with this one. . . ." The figure moved. "But this one goes where? And this one?"

"Let be," said his wife. The figure sat up slowly and rolled its eyes loosely.

"Listen, Reb *Golem,*" the old man said, wagging his finger. "Pay attention to what I say—you understand?"

"Understand. . . ."

"If you want to stay here, you got to do like Mr. Gumbeiner says."

"Do-like-Mr.-Gumbeiner-says. . . ."

"That's the way I like to hear a *golem* talk. Malka, give here the mirror from the pocketbook. Look, you see your face? You see on the forehead, what's written? If you don't do like Mr. Gumbeiner says, he'll wipe out what's written and you'll be no more alive."

"No-more-alive. . . ."

"That's right. Now, listen. Under the porch you'll find a lawnmower. Take it. And cut the lawn. Then come back. Go."

"Go. . . ." The figure shambled down the stairs. Presently the sound of the lawnmower whirred through the quiet air in the street just like the street where Jackie Cooper shed huge tears on Wallace Beery's shirt and Chester Conklin rolled his eyes at Marie Dressler.

"So what will you write to Tillie?" old Mr. Gumbeiner asked.

"What should I write?" old Mrs. Gumbeiner shrugged. "I'll write that the weather is lovely out here and that we are both, Blessed be the Name, in good health."

The old man nodded his head slowly, and they sat together on the front porch in the warm afternoon sun.

Now we return to the question of identity, which appears so often that I suspect it is one of the ground notes of imaginative fiction. Most of the stories in this book, in fact, are about the nature of reality in one aspect or another. In "They," in "C/o Mr. Makepeace," and in this story, it takes the most agonizing form of all. "I think, therefore I exist": but *who* am I? On the bright side, in the hemisphere of daylight, clarity, and good common sense, it is tacitly agreed that this question shall not be asked. But in dreams, in drunkenness, in moments of shock and strong emotion, each of us, at some time in his life, must come face to face with it.

H. G. Wells

THE STORY
OF THE LATE
MR. ELVESHAM

I set this story down, not expecting it will be believed, but, if possible, to prepare a way of escape for the next victim. He perhaps may profit by my misfortune. My own case, I know, is hopeless, and I am now in some measure prepared to meet my fate.

My name is Edward George Eden. I was born at Trentham, in Staffordshire, my father being employed in the gardens there. I lost my mother when I was three years old and my father when I was five, my uncle, George Eden, then adopting me as his own son. He was a single man, self-educated, and well-known in Birmingham as an enterprising journalist; he educated me generously, fired my ambition to succeed in the world, and at his death, which happened four years ago, left me his entire fortune, a matter of about five hundred pounds after all outgoing charges were paid. I was then eighteen. He advised me in his will to expend the money in completing my education. I had already chosen the profession of medicine, and through his posthumous generosity, and my good fortune in a scholarship competition, I became a medical student at University College, London. At the time of the beginning of my story I lodged at 11A University Street, in a little upper room, very shabbily furnished, and draughty, overlooking the back of Shoolbred's premises. I used this little room both to live in and sleep in, because I was anxious to eke out my means to the very last shilling's-worth.

I was taking a pair of shoes to be mended at a shop in the Tottenham Court Road when I first encountered the little old man with the yellow face, with whom my life has now become so inextricably entangled. He was standing on the kerb, and staring at the number on the door in a doubtful way, as I opened it. His eyes—they were dull grey eyes, and reddish under the rims—fell to my face, and his countenance immediately assumed an expression of corrugated amiability.

"You come," he said, "apt to the moment. I had forgotten the number of your house. How do you do, Mr. Eden?"

I was a little astonished at his familiar address, for I had never set eyes on the man before. I was annoyed, too, at his catching me with my boots under my arm. He noticed my lack of cordiality.

"Wonder who the deuce I am, eh? A friend, let me assure you. I have seen you before, though you haven't seen me. Is there anywhere where I can talk to you?"

I hesitated. The shabbiness of my room upstairs was not a matter for every stranger. "Perhaps," said I, "we might walk down the street. I'm unfortunately prevented—" My gesture explained the sentence before I had spoken it.

"The very thing," he said, and faced this way and then that. "The street? Which way shall we go?" I slipped my boots down in the passage. "Look here!" he said abruptly, "this business of mine is a rigmarole. Come and lunch with me, Mr. Eden. I'm an old man, a very old man, and not good at explanations, and what with my piping voice and the clatter of the traffic—"

He laid a persuasive skinny hand that trembled a little upon my arm.

I was not so old that an old man might not treat me to a lunch. Yet at the same time I was not altogether pleased by this abrupt invitation. "I had rather—" I began. "But *I* had rather," he said, catching me up, "and a certain civility is surely due to my grey hairs," and so I consented, and went away with him.

He took me to Blavitski's; I had to walk slowly to accommodate myself to his pace; and over such a lunch as I had never tasted before, he fended off my leading questions, and I took a better note of his appearance. His clean-shaven face was lean and wrinkled, his shrivelled lips fell over a set of false teeth, and his white hair was thin and rather long; he seemed small to me—though, indeed, most people seemed small to me—and his shoulders were rounded and bent. And, watching him, I could not help but observe that he, too, was taking note of me, running his eyes, with a curious touch of greed in them, over me from my broad shoulders to my suntanned hands and up to my freckled face again. "And now," said he, as we lit our cigarettes, "I must tell you of the business in hand.

"I must tell you, then, that I am an old man, a very old man." He paused momentarily. "And it happens that I have money that I must presently be leaving, and never a child have I to leave it to." I thought of the confidence trick, and resolved I would be on the alert for the vestiges of my five hundred pounds. He proceeded to enlarge on his loneliness, and the trouble he had to find a proper disposition of his money. "I have weighed this plan and that plan, charities, institutions, and scholarships, and libraries, and I have come to this conclusion at last,"—he fixed his eyes on my face—"that I will find some young fellow, ambitious, pure-minded, and poor, healthy in body and healthy in mind, and, in short, make him my heir, give him all that I have." He repeated, "Give him all that I have. So that he will suddenly be lifted out of all the trouble and struggle in which his sympathies have been educated, to freedom and influence."

I tried to seem disinterested. With a transparent hypocrisy, I said, "And you want my help, my professional services maybe, to find that person."

He smiled, and looked at me over his cigarette, and I laughed at his quiet exposure of my modest pretence.

"What a career such a man might have!" he said. "It fills me with envy to think how I have accumulated that another man may spend—

"But there are conditions, of course, burdens to be imposed. He must, for instance, take my name. You cannot expect everything without some return. And I must go into all the circumstances of his life before I can accept him. He *must* be sound. I must know his heredity, how his parents and grandparents died, have the strictest inquiries made into his private morals—"

This modified my secret congratulations a little. "And do I understand," said I, "that I—?"

"Yes," he said, almost fiercely. "You. *You*."

I answered never a word. My imagination was dancing wildly, my innate scepticism was useless to modify its transports. There was not a particle of gratitude in my mind—I did not know what to say nor how to say it. "But why me in particular?" I said at last.

He had chanced to hear of me from Professor Haslar, he said, as a typically sound and sane young man, and he wished, as far as possible, to leave his money where health and integrity were assured.

That was my first meeting with the little old man. He was mysterious about himself; he would not give his name yet, he said, and after I had answered some questions of his, he left me at the Blavitski portal. I noticed that he drew a handful of gold coins from his pocket when it came to paying for the lunch. His insistence upon bodily health was curious. In accordance with an arrangement we had made I applied that day for a life policy in the Loyal Insurance Company for a large sum, and I was exhaustively overhauled by the medical advisers of that company in the subsequent week. Even that did not satisfy him, and he insisted I must be re-examined by the great Doctor Henderson. It was Friday in Whitsun week before he came to a decision. He called me down quite late in the evening—nearly nine it was—from cramming chemical equations for my Preliminary Scientific examination. He was standing in the passage under the feeble gas lamp, and his face was a grotesque interplay of shadows. He seemed more bowed than when I had first seen him, and his cheeks had sunk in a little.

His voice shook with emotion. "Everything is satisfactory, Mr. Eden," he said. "Everything is quite, quite satisfactory. And this night of all nights, you must dine with me and celebrate your—accession." He was interrupted by a cough. "You won't have long to wait, either," he said, wiping his handkerchief across his lips, and gripping my hand with his long bony claw that was disengaged. "Certainly not very long to wait."

We went into the street and called a cab. I remember every incident of that drive vividly, the swift, easy motion, the contrast of gas and oil and electric light, the crowds of people in the streets, the place in Regent Street to which we went, and the sumptuous dinner we were served with there. I was disconcerted at first by the well-dressed waiter's glances at my rough clothes, bothered by the stones of the olives, but as the champagne warmed my blood, my confidence revived. At first the old man talked of himself. He had already told me his name in the cab; he was Egbert Elvesham, the great philosopher, whose name I had known since I was a lad at school. It seemed incredible to me that this man, whose intelligence had so early dominated mine, this great abstraction should suddenly realise itself as this decrepit, familiar figure. I daresay every young fellow who has suddenly fallen among celebrities has felt something of my disappointment. He told me now of the future that the feeble streams of his life would presently leave dry for me, houses, copyrights, investments; I had never suspected that philosophers were so rich. He watched me drink and eat with a touch of envy. "What a capacity for living you have!" he said; and then, with a sigh, a sigh of relief I could have thought it, "It will not be long."

"Ay," said I, my head swimming now with champagne; "I have a future perhaps—of a fairly agreeable sort, thanks to you. I shall now have the honour of your name. But you have a past. Such a past as is worth all my future."

He shook his head and smiled, as I thought with half-sad appreciation of my flattering admiration. "That future," he said, "would you in truth change it?" The waiter came with liqueurs. "You will not perhaps mind taking my name, taking my position, but would you indeed—willingly—take my years?"

"With your achievements," said I gallantly.

He smiled again. "Kümmel—both," he said to the waiter, and turned his attention to a little paper packet he had taken from his pocket. "This hour," said he, "this after-dinner hour is the hour of small things. Here is a scrap of my unpublished wisdom." He opened the packet with his shaking yellow fingers, and showed a little pinkish powder on the paper. "This," said he—"well, you must guess what it is. But Kümmel—put but a dash of this powder in it—is Himmel." His large greyish eyes watched mine with an inscrutable expression.

It was a bit of a shock to me to find this great teacher gave his mind to the flavour of liqueurs. However, I feigned a great interest in his weakness, for I was drunk enough for such small sycophancy.

He parted the powder between the little glasses, and rising suddenly with a strange unexpected dignity, held out his hand towards me. I imitated his action, and the glasses rang. "To a quick succession," said he, and raised his glass towards his lips.

"Not that," I said hastily. "Not that."

He paused, with the liqueur at the level of his chin, and his eyes blazing into mine.

"To a long life," said I.

He hesitated. "To a long life," said he, with a sudden bark of laughter, and with eyes fixed on one another we tilted the little glasses. His eyes looked straight into mine, and as I drained the stuff off, I felt a curiously intense sensation. The first touch of it set my brain in a furious tumult; I seemed to feel an actual physical stirring in my skull, and a seething humming filled my ears. I did not notice the flavour in my mouth, the aroma that filled my throat; I saw only the grey intensity of his gaze that burnt into mine. The draught, the mental confusion, the noise and stirring in my head, seemed to last an interminable time. Curious vague impressions of half-forgotten things danced and vanished on the edge of my consciousness. At last he broke the spell. With a sudden explosive sigh he put down his glass.

"Well?" he said.

"It's glorious," said I, though I had not tasted the stuff.

My head was spinning. I sat down. My brain was chaos. Then my perception grew clear and minute as though I saw things in a concave mirror. His manner seemed to have changed into something nervous and hasty. He pulled out his watch and grimaced at it. "Eleven-seven! And tonight I must—Seven—twenty-five. Waterloo! I must go at once." He called for the bill, and struggled with his coat. Officious waiters came to our assistance. In another moment I was wishing him goodbye, over the apron of a cab, and still with an absurd feeling of minute distinctness, as though—how can I express it?—I not only saw but *felt* through an inverted opera-glass.

"That stuff," he said. He put his hand to his forehead. "I ought not to have given it to you. It will make your head split tomorrow. Wait a minute. Here." He handed me out a little flat thing like a seidlitz-powder. "Take that in water as you are going to bed. The other thing was a drug. Not till you're ready to go to bed, mind. It will clear your head. That's all. One more shake—Futurus!"

I gripped his shrivelled claw. "Goodbye," he said, and by

the droop of his eyelids I judged he, too, was a little under the influence of that brain-twisting cordial.

He recollected something else with a start, felt in his breast-pocket, and produced another packet, this time a cylinder the size and shape of a shaving-stick. "Here," said he. "I'd almost forgotten. Don't open this until I come to-morrow—but take it now."

It was so heavy that I well nigh dropped it. "All ri'!" said I, and he grinned at me through the cab window, as the cab-man flicked his horse into wakefulness. It was a white packet he had given me, with red seals at either end and along its edge. "If this isn't money," said I, "it's platinum or lead."

I stuck it with elaborate care into my pocket, and with a whirling brain walked home through the Regent Street loi-terers and the dark back streets beyond Portland Road. I remember the sensations of that walk very vividly, strange as they were. I was still so far myself that I could notice my strange mental state, and wonder whether this stuff I had had was opium—a drug beyond my experience. It is hard now to describe the peculiarity of my mental strangeness—mental doubling vaguely expresses it. As I was walking up Regent Street I found in my mind a queer persuasion that it was Waterloo station, and had an odd impulse to get into the Polytechnic as a man might get into a train. I put a knuckle in my eye, and it was Regent Street. How can I express it? You see a skillful actor looking quietly at you, he pulls a grimace, and lo!—another person. Is it too ex-travagant if I tell you that it seemed to me as if Regent Street had, for the moment, done that? Then, being persuaded it was Regent Street again, I was oddly muddled about some fantastic reminiscences that cropped up. "Thirty years ago," thought I, "it was here that I quarrelled with my brother." Then I burst out laughing, to the astonishment and encouragement of a group of night prowlers. Thirty years ago I did not exist, and never in my life had I boasted a brother. The stuff was surely liquid folly, for the poignant regret for that lost brother still clung to me. Along Portland Road the madness took another turn. I began to recall vanished shops, and to compare the street with what it used to be. Confused, troubled thinking was comprehensible enough after the drink I had taken, but what puzzled me were these curiously vivid phantasmal memories that had crept into my mind; and not only the memories that had crept in, but also the memories that had slipped out. I stopped opposite Stevens', the natural history dealer's, and cudgelled my brains to think what he had to do with me. A 'bus went by, and sounded exactly like the rumbling of a train. I seemed to be dipped into some dark, remote pit for the recollection. "Of course," said I, at last, "he has promised me three frogs tomorrow. Odd I should have forgotten."

Do they still show children dissolving views? In those I remember one view would begin like a faint ghost, and grow and oust another. In just that way it seemed to me that a ghostly set of new sensations was struggling with those of my ordinary self.

I went on through Euston Road to Tottenham Court Road, puzzled and a little frightened, and scarcely noticed the unusual way I was taking, for commonly I used to cut through the intervening network of back streets. I turned into University Street, to discover that I had forgotten my number. Only by a strong effort did I recall 11A, and even then it seemed to me that it was a thing some forgotten person had told me. I tried to steady my mind by recalling the incidents of the dinner, and for the life of me I could conjure up no picture of my host's face; I saw him only as a shadowy outline, as one might see oneself reflected in a window through which one was looking. In his place, however, I had a curious exterior vision of myself sitting at a table, flushed, bright-eyed, and talkative.

"I must take this other powder," said I. "This is getting impossible."

I tried the wrong side of the hall for my candle and the matches, and had a doubt of which landing my room might be on. "I'm drunk," I said, "that's certain," and blundered needlessly on the staircase to sustain the proposition.

At the first glance my room seemed unfamiliar. "What rot!" I said, and stared about me. I seemed to bring myself back by the effort and the odd phantasmal quality passed into the concrete familiar. There was the old looking-glass, with my notes on the albumens stuck in the corner of the frame, my old everyday suit of clothes pitched about the floor. And yet it was not so real, after all. I felt an idiotic persuasion trying to creep into my mind, as it were, that I was in a railway carriage in a train just stopping, that I was peering out of the window at some unknown station. I gripped the bedrail firmly to reassure myself. "It's clairvoyance, perhaps," I said. "I must write to the Psychical Research Society."

I put the rouleau on my dressing-table, sat on my bed and began to take off my boots. It was as if the picture of my present sensations was painted over some other picture that was trying to show through. "Curse it!" said I; "my wits are going, or am I in two places at once?" Half-undressed,

I tossed the powder into a glass and drank it off. It effervesced, and became a fluorescent amber colour. Before I was in bed my mind was already tranquillised. I felt the pillow at my cheek, and thereupon I must have fallen asleep.

I awoke abruptly out of a dream of strange beasts, and found myself lying on my back. Probably everyone knows that dismal emotional dream from which one escapes, awake indeed but strangely cowed. There was a curious taste in my mouth, a tired feeling in my limbs, a sense of cutaneous discomfort. I lay with my head motionless on my pillow, expecting that my feeling of strangeness and terror would probably pass away, and that I should then doze off again to sleep. But instead of that, my uncanny sensations increased. At first I could perceive nothing wrong about me. There was a faint light in the room, so faint that it was the very next thing to darkness, and the furniture stood out in it as vague blots of absolute darkness. I stared with my eyes just over the bedclothes.

It came into my mind that someone had entered the room to rob me of my rouleau of money, but after lying for some moments, breathing regularly to simulate sleep, I realised this was mere fancy. Nevertheless, the uneasy assurance of something wrong kept fast hold of me. With an effort I raised my head from the pillow, and peered about me at the dark. What it was I could not conceive. I looked at the dim shapes around me, the greater and lesser darknesses that indicated curtains, table, fireplace, bookshelves, and so forth. Then I began to perceive something unfamiliar in the forms of the darkness. Had the bed turned round? Yonder should be the bookshelves, and something shrouded and pallid rose there, something that would not answer to the bookshelves, however I looked at it. It was far too big to be my shirt thrown on a chair.

Overcoming a childish terror, I threw back the bedclothes and thrust my leg out of bed. I found my foot scarcely reached the edge of the mattress. I made another step, as it were, and sat up on the edge of the bed. By the side of my bed should be the candle, and the matches upon the broken chair. I put out my hand and touched—nothing. I waved my hand in the darkness, and it came against some heavy hanging, soft and thick in texture, which gave a rustling noise at my touch. I grasped this and pulled it; it appeared to be a curtain suspended over the head of my bed.

I was now thoroughly awake, and beginning to realise that I was in a strange room. I was puzzled. I tried to recall the overnight circumstances, and I found them now, curiously enough, vivid in my memory: the supper, my reception of the little packages, my wonder whether I was intoxicated, my slow undressing, the coolness to my flushed face of my pillow. I felt a sudden distrust. Was that last night, or the night before? At any rate, this room was strange to me, and I could not imagine how I had got into it. The dim, pallid outline was growing paler, and I perceived it was a window, with the dark shape of an oval toilet-glass against the weak intimation of the dawn that filtered through the blind. I stood up, and was surprised by a curious feeling of weakness and unsteadiness. With trembling hands outstretched, I walked slowly towards the window, getting, nevertheless, a bruise on the knee from a chair by the way. I fumbled round the glass, which was

large, with handsome brass sconces, to find the blind-cord.
I could not find any. By chance I took hold of the tassel,
and with the click of a spring the blind ran up.

I found myself looking out upon a scene that was altogether strange to me. The night was overcast, and through
the flocculent grey of the heaped clouds there filtered a faint
half-light of dawn. Just at the edge of the sky, the cloud-
canopy had a blood-red rim. Below, everything was dark
and indistinct, dim hills in the distance, a vague mass of
buildings running up into pinnacles, trees like spilt ink, and
below the window a tracery of black bushes and pale grey
paths. It was so unfamiliar that for the moment I thought
myself still dreaming. I felt the toilet-table; it appeared to be
made of some polished wood, and was rather elaborately
furnished—there were little cut-glass bottles and a brush
upon it. There was also a queer little object, horseshoe-
shaped it felt, with smooth, hard projections, lying in a
saucer. I could find no matches nor candle-stick.

I turned my eyes to the room again. Now the blind was
up, faint spectres of its furnishing came out of the darkness.
There was a huge curtained bed, and the fireplace at its foot
had a large white mantel with something of the shimmer of
marble.

I leant against the toilet-table, shut my eyes and opened
them again, and tried to think. The whole thing was far too
real for dreaming. I was inclined to imagine there was still
some hiatus in my memory as a consequence of my draught
of that strange liqueur; that I had come into my inheritance,
perhaps, and suddenly lost my recollection of everything
since my good fortune had been announced. Perhaps if I
waited a little, things would be clearer to me again. Yet my

dinner with old Elvesham was now singularly vivid and recent. The champagne, the observant waiters, the powder, and the liqueurs—I could have staked my soul it all happened a few hours ago.

And then occurred a thing so trivial and yet so terrible to me that I shiver now to think of that moment. I spoke aloud. I said, "How the devil did I get here?" . . . *And the voice was not my own.*

It was not my own, it was thin, the articulation was slurred, the resonance of my facial bones was different. Then to reassure myself I ran one hand over the other, and felt loose folds of skin, the bony laxity of age. "Surely," I said in that horrible voice that had somehow established itself in my throat, "surely this thing is a dream!" Almost as quickly as if I did it involuntarily, I thrust my fingers into my mouth. My teeth had gone. My finger-tips ran on the flaccid surface of an even row of shrivelled gums. I was sick with dismay and disgust.

I felt then a passionate desire to see myself, to realise at once in its full horror the ghastly change that had come upon me. I tottered to the mantel, and felt along it for matches. As I did so, a barking cough sprang up in my throat, and I clutched the thick flannel nightdress I found about me. There were no matches there, and I suddenly realised that my extremities were cold. Sniffing and coughing, whimpering a little perhaps, I fumbled back to bed. "It is surely a dream," I whimpered to myself as I clambered back, "surely a dream." It was a senile repetition. I pulled the bedclothes over my shoulders, over my ears. I thrust my withered hand under the pillow, and determined to compose myself to sleep. Of course it was a dream. In the morning the dream would be over, and I should wake up strong and vigorous again to my youth and studies. I shut my eyes, breathed regularly, and, finding myself wakeful, began to count slowly through the powers of three.

But the thing I desired would not come. I could not get to sleep. And the persuasion of the inexorable reality of the change that had happened to me grew steadily. Presently I found myself with my eyes wide open, the powers of three forgotten, and my skinny fingers upon my shrivelled gums. I was indeed, suddenly and abruptly, an old man. I had in some unaccountable manner fallen through my life and come to old age, in some way I had been cheated of all the best of my life, of love, of struggle, of strength and hope. I grovelled into the pillow and tried to persuade myself that such hallucination was possible. Imperceptibly, steadily, the dawn grew clearer.

At last, despairing of further sleep, I sat up in bed and looked about me. A chill twilight rendered the whole chamber visible. It was spacious and well-furnished, better furnished than any room I had ever slept in before. A candle and matches became dimly visible upon a little pedestal in a recess. I threw back the bedclothes, and shivering with the rawness of the early morning, albeit it was summer-time, I got out and lit the candle. Then, trembling horribly so that the extinguisher rattled on its spike, I tottered to the glass and saw—*Elvesham's face!* It was none the less horrible because I had already dimly feared as much. He had already seemed physically weak and pitiful to me, but seen now, dressed only in a coarse flannel nightdress that fell apart and showed the stringy neck, seen now as my own body, I cannot describe its desolate decrepitude. The hollow cheeks, the straggling tail of dirty grey hair, the rheumy bleared eyes, the quivering, shrivelled lips, the lower displaying a gleam of the pink interior lining, and those horrible dark gums showing. You who are mind and body together at your natural years, cannot imagine what this fiendish imprisonment meant to me. To be young, and full of the desire and energy of youth, and to be caught, and presently to be crushed in this tottering ruin of a body. . . .

But I wander from the course of my story. For some time I must have been stunned at this change that had come upon me. It was daylight when I did so far gather myself together as to think. In some inexplicable way I had been changed, though how, short of magic, the thing had been done, I could not say. And as I thought, the diabolical ingenuity of Elvesham came home to me. It seemed plain to me that as I found myself in his, so he must be in possession of *my* body, of my strength that is, and my future. But how to prove it? Then as I thought, the thing became so incredible even to me that my mind reeled, and I had to pinch myself, to feel my toothless gums, to see myself in the glass, and touch the things about me before I could steady myself to face the facts again. Was all life hallucination? Was I indeed Elvesham, and he me? Had I been dreaming of Eden overnight? Was there any Eden? But if I was Elvesham, I should remember where I was on the previous morning, the name of the town in which I lived, what happened before the dream began. I struggled with my thoughts. I recalled the queer doubleness of my memories overnight. But now my mind was clear. Not the ghost of any memories but those proper to Eden could I raise.

"This way lies insanity!" I cried in my piping voice. I staggered to my feet, dragged my feeble, heavy limbs to the washhand-stand, and plunged my grey head into a basin of cold water. Then, towelling myself, I tried again. It was no good. I felt beyond all question that I was indeed Eden, not Elvesham. But Eden in Elvesham's body!

Had I been a man of any other age, I might have given myself up to my fate as one enchanted. But in these sceptical days miracles do not pass current. Here was some trick of psychology. What a drug and a steady stare could do, a drug and a steady stare, or some similar treatment, could surely undo. Men have lost their memories before. But to exchange memories as one does umbrellas! I laughed. Alas! not a healthy laugh, but a wheezing, senile titter. I could have fancied old Elvesham laughing at my plight, and a gust of petulant anger, unusual to me, swept across my feelings. I began dressing eagerly in the clothes I found lying about on the floor, and only realised when I was dressed that it was an evening suit I had assumed. I opened the wardrobe and found some ordinary clothes, a pair of plaid trousers, and an old-fashioned dressing-gown. I put a venerable smoking-cap on my venerable head, and, coughing a little from my exertions, tottered out upon the landing.

It was then perhaps a quarter to six, and the blinds were closely drawn and the house quite silent. The landing was a spacious one, a broad, richly-carpeted staircase went down into the darkness of the hall below, and before me a door ajar showed me a writing-desk, a revolving bookcase, the back of a study chair, and a fine array of bound books, shelf upon shelf.

"My study," I mumbled, and walked across the landing.

Then at the sound of my voice a thought struck me, and I went back to the bedroom and put in the set of false teeth. They slipped in with the ease of old habit. "That's better," said I, gnashing them, and so returned to the study.

The drawers of the writing-desk were locked. Its revolving top was also locked. I could see no indications of the keys, and there were none in the pockets of my trousers. I shuffled back at once to the bedroom, and went through the dress suit, and afterwards the pockets of all the garments I could find. I was very eager; and one might have imagined that burglars had been at work, to see my room when I had done. Not only were there no keys to be found, but not a coin, nor a scrap of paper—save only the receipted bill of the overnight dinner.

A curious weariness asserted itself. I sat down and stared at the garments flung here and there, their pockets turned inside out. My first frenzy had already flickered out. Every moment I was beginning to realise the immense intelligence of the plans of my enemy, to see more and more clearly the hopelessness of my position. With an effort I rose and hurried into the study again. On the staircase was a housemaid pulling up the blinds. She stared, I think, at the expression of my face. I shut the door of the study behind me, and, seizing a poker, began an attack upon the desk. That is how they found me. The cover of the desk was split, the lock smashed, the letters torn out of the pigeon-holes and tossed about the room. In my senile rage I had flung about the pens and other such light stationery, and overturned the ink. Moreover, a large vase upon the mantel had got broken—I do not know how. I could find no cheque-book, no money, no indications of the slightest use for the recovery of my body. I was battering madly at the drawers, when the butler, backed by two women-servants, intruded upon me.

That simply is the story of my change. No one will believe my frantic assertions. I am treated as one demented, and even at this moment I am under restraint. But I am sane, absolutely sane, and to prove it I have sat down to write this story minutely as the thing happened to me. I appeal to the reader, whether there is any trace of insanity in the style or method of the story he has been reading. I am a young man locked away in an old man's body. But the clear fact is incredible to everyone. Naturally I appear demented to those who will not believe this, naturally I do not know the names of my secretaries, of the doctors who come to see me, of my servants and neighbours, of this town (wherever it is) where I find myself. Naturally I lose myself in my own house, and suffer inconveniences of every sort. Naturally I ask the oddest questions. Naturally I weep and cry out, and have paroxysms of despair. I have no money and no cheque-book. The bank will not recognise my signature, for I suppose that, allowing for the feeble muscles I now have, my handwriting is still Eden's. These people about me will not let me go to the bank personally. It seems, indeed, that there is no bank in this town, and that I have taken an account in some part of London. It seems that Elvesham kept the name of his solicitor secret from all his household—I can ascertain nothing. Elvesham was, of course, a profound student of mental science, and all my declarations of the facts of the case merely confirm the theory that my insanity is the outcome of over-much brooding upon psychology. Dreams of the personal identity indeed! Two days ago I was a healthy youngster, with all life before me; now I am a furious old man, unkempt and desperate and miserable, prowling about a great luxurious strange house, watched, feared, and avoided as a lunatic by everyone about me. And in London is Elvesham beginning life again in a vigorous body, and with all the accumulated knowledge and wisdom of threescore and ten. He has stolen my life.

What has happened I do not clearly know. In the study are volumes of manuscript notes referring chiefly to the psychology of memory, and parts of what may be either calculations or ciphers in symbols absolutely strange to me. In some passages there are indications that he was also occupied with the philosophy of mathematics. I take it he has transferred the whole of his memories, the accumulation that makes up his personality, from this old withered brain of his to mine, and, similarly, that he has transferred mine to his discarded tenement. Practically, that is, he has changed bodies. But how such a change may be possible is without the range of my philosophy. I have been a materialist for all my thinking life, but here, suddenly, is a clear case of man's detachability from matter.

One desperate experiment I am about to try. I sit writing here before putting the matter to issue. This morning, with the help of a table-knife that I had secreted at breakfast, I succeeded in breaking open a fairly obvious secret drawer in this wrecked writing-desk. I discovered nothing save a little green glass phial containing a white powder. Round the neck of the phial was a label, and thereon was written this one word: *"Release."* This may be—is most probably, poison. I can understand Elvesham placing poison in my way, and I should be sure that it was his intention so to get rid of the only living witness against him were it not for this careful concealment. The man has practically solved the problem of immortality. Save for the spite of chance, he will live in my body until it has aged, and then, again, throwing that aside, he will assume some other victim's youth and strength. When one remembers his heartlessness, it is terrible to think of the ever-growing experience, that . . . How long has he been leaping from body to body? . . . But I tire of writing. The powder appears to be soluble in water. The taste is not unpleasant.

There the narrative found upon Mr. Elvesham's desk ends. His dead body lay between the desk and the chair. The latter had been pushed back, probably by his last convulsions. The story was written in pencil, and in a crazy hand quite unlike his usual minute characters. There remain only two curious facts to record. Indisputably there was some connection between Eden and Elvesham, since the whole of Elvesham's property was bequeathed to the young man. But he never inherited. When Elvesham committed suicide, Eden was, strangely enough, already dead. Twenty-four hours before, he had been knocked down by a cab and killed instantly, at the crowded crossing at the intersection of Gower Street and Euston Road. So that the only human being who could have thrown light upon this fantastic narrative is beyond the reach of questions.

Here is the second of our two stories on the Frankenstein theme. This one is pure nightmare-stuff, with just enough admixture of waking reality to hold it together. It has the curious, compelling quality of dream, in which opposites do not cancel out but reinforce each other. Like *Frankenstein,* this is the story of a monster who is dead but alive, evil but innocent. It touches a deep nerve; I think I can promise you will not forget it.

Theodore Sturgeon

IT

It walked in the woods.

It was never born. It existed. Under the pine needles the fires burn, deep and smokeless in the mold. In heat and in darkness and decay there is growth. There is life and there is growth. It grew, but it was not alive. It walked unbreathing through the woods, and thought and saw and was hideous and strong, and it was not born and it did not live. It grew and moved about without living.

It crawled out of the darkness and hot damp mold into the cool of the morning. It was huge. It was lumped and crusted with its own hateful substances, and pieces of it dropped off as it went its way, dropped off and lay writhing, and stilled, and sank putrescent into the forest loam.

It had no mercy, no laughter, no beauty. It had strength and great intelligence. And—perhaps it could not be destroyed. It crawled out of its mound in the wood and lay pulsing in the sunlight for a long moment. Patches of it shone wetly in the golden glow, parts of it were nubbled and flaked. And whose dead bones had given it the form of a man?

It scrabbled painfully with its half-formed hands, beating the ground and the bole of a tree. It rolled and lifted itself up on its crumbling elbows, and it tore up a great handful of herbs and shredded them against its chest, and it paused and gazed at the gray-green juices with intelligent calm. It wavered to its feet, and seized a young sapling and destroyed it, folding the slender trunk back on itself again and again, watching attentively the useless, fibered splinters. And it squealed, snatching up a fear-frozen field-creature, crushing it slowly, letting blood and pulpy flesh and fur ooze from between its fingers, run down and rot on the forearms.

It began searching.

Kimbo drifted through the tall grasses like a puff of dust, his bushy tail curled tightly over his back and his long jaws agape. He ran with an easy lope, loving his freedom and the power of his flanks and furry shoulders. His tongue lolled listlessly over his lips. His lips were black and serrated, and each tiny pointed liplet swayed with his doggy gallop. Kimbo was all dog, all healthy animal.

He leaped high over a boulder and landed with a startled yelp as a long-eared cony shot from its hiding place under the rock. Kimbo hurtled after it, grunting with each great thrust of his legs. The rabbit bounced just ahead of him, keeping its distance, its ears flattened on its curving back and its little legs nibbling away at distance hungrily. It stopped, and Kimbo pounced, and the rabbit shot away at a tangent and popped into a hollow log. Kimbo yelped again and rushed snuffling at the log, and knowing his failure, curvetted but once around the stump and ran on into the forest. The thing that watched from the wood raised its crusted arms and waited for Kimbo.

Kimbo sensed it there, standing dead-still by the path.

To him it was a bulk which smelled of carrion not fit to roll in, and he snuffled distastefully and ran to pass it.

The thing let him come abreast and dropped a heavy twisted fist on him. Kimbo saw it coming and curled up tight as he ran, and the hand clipped stunningly on his rump, sending him rolling and yipping down the slope. Kimbo straddled to his feet, shook his head, shook his body with a deep growl, came back to the silent thing with green murder in his eyes. He walked stiffly, straight-legged, his tail as low as his lowered head and a ruff of fury round his neck. The thing raised its arms again, waited.

Kimbo slowed, then flipped himself through the air at the monster's throat. His jaws closed on it; his teeth clicked together through a mass of filth, and he fell choking and snarling at its feet. The thing leaned down and struck twice, and after the dog's back was broken, it sat beside him and began to tear him apart.

"Be back in an hour or so," said Alton Drew, picking up his rifle from the corner behind the wood box. His brother laughed.

"Old Kimbo 'bout runs your life, Alton," he said.

"Ah, I know the ol' devil," said Alton. "When I whistle for him for half an hour and he don't show up, he's in a jam or he's treed something wuth shootin' at. The ol' son of a gun calls me by not answerin'."

Cory Drew shoved a full glass of milk over to his nine-year-old daughter and smiled. "You think as much o' that houn'-dog o' yours as I do of Babe here."

Babe slid off her chair and ran to her uncle. "Gonna catch me the bad fella, Uncle Alton?" she shrilled. The

"bad fella" was Cory's invention—the one who lurked in
corners ready to pounce on little girls who chased the chickens and played around mowing machines and hurled green
apples with a powerful young arm at the sides of the hogs,
to hear the synchronized thud and grunt; little girls who
swore with an Austrian accent like an ex-hired man they
had had; who dug caves in haystacks till they tipped over,
and kept pet crawfish in tomorrow's milk cans, and rode
work horses to a lather in the night pasture.

"Get back here and keep away from Uncle Alton's gun!"
said Cory. "If you see the bad fella, Alton, chase him back
here. He has a date with Babe here for that stunt of hers
last night." The preceding evening, Babe had kindheartedly
poured pepper on the cows' salt block.

"Don't worry, kiddo," grinned her uncle, "I'll bring you
the bad fella's hide if he don't get me first."

Alton Drew walked up the path toward the wood, thinking
about Babe. She was a phenomenon—a pampered farm
child. Ah, well—she had to be. They'd both loved Clissa
Drew, and she'd married Cory, and they had to love Clissa's
child. Funny thing, love. Alton was a man's man, and
thought things out that way; and his reaction to love was
a strong and frightened one. He knew what love was because
he felt it still for his brother's wife and would feel it as long
as he lived for Babe. It led him through his life, and yet he
embarrassed himself by thinking of it. Loving a dog was an
easy thing, because you and the old devil could love one
another completely without talking about it. The smell of
gun smoke and the smell of wet fur in the rain were perfume
enough for Alton Drew, a grunt of satisfaction and the

scream of something hunted and hit were poetry enough. They weren't like love for a human, that choked his throat so he could not say words he could not have thought of anyway. So Alton loved his dog Kimbo and his Winchester for all to see, and let his love for his brother's women, Clissa and Babe, eat at him quietly and unmentioned.

His quick eyes saw the fresh indentations in the soft earth behind the boulder, which showed where Kimbo had turned and leaped with a single surge, chasing the rabbit. Ignoring the tracks, he looked for the nearest place where a rabbit might hide, and strolled over to the stump. Kimbo had been there, he saw, and had been there too late. "You're an ol' fool," muttered Alton. "Y' can't catch a cony by chasin' it. You want to cross him up some way." He gave a peculiar trilling whistle, sure that Kimbo was digging frantically under some nearby stump for a rabbit that was three counties away by now. No answer. A little puzzled, Alton went back to the path. "He never done this before," he said softly. There was something about this he didn't like.

He cocked his .32-40 and cradled it. At the county fair someone had once said of Alton Drew that he could shoot at a handful of salt and pepper thrown in the air and hit only the pepper. Once he split a bullet on the blade of a knife and put two candles out. He had no need to fear anything that could be shot at. That's what he believed.

The thing in the woods looked curiously down at what it had done to Kimbo, and moaned the way Kimbo had before he died. It stood a minute storing away facts in its foul, unemotional mind. Blood was warm. The sunlight was warm. Things that moved and bore fur had a muscle to force the thick liquid through tiny tubes in their bodies. The liquid coagulated after a time. The liquid on rooted green things was thinner and the loss of a limb did not mean loss of life. It was very interesting, but the thing, the mold with a mind, was not pleased. Neither was it displeased. Its accidental urge was a thirst for knowledge, and it was only —interested.

It was growing late, and the sun reddened and rested awhile on the hilly horizon, teaching the clouds to be inverted flames. The thing threw up its head suddenly, noticing the dusk. Night was ever a strange thing, even for those of us who have known it in life. It would have been frightening for the monster had it been capable of fright, but it could only be curious; it could only reason from what it had observed.

What was happening? It was getting harder to see. Why? It threw its shapeless head from side to side. It was true— things were dim, and growing dimmer. Things were changing shape, taking on a new and darker color. What did the creatures it had crushed and torn apart see? How did they see? The larger one, the one that had attacked, had used two organs in its head. That must have been it, because after the thing had torn off two of the dog's legs it had struck at the hairy muzzle; and the dog, seeing the blow coming, had dropped folds of skin over the organs—closed its eyes. Ergo, the dog saw with its eyes. But then after the dog was dead, and its body still, repeated blows had had no effect on the eyes. They remained open and staring. The logical conclusion was, then, that a being that had ceased

to live and breathe and move about lost the use of its eyes.
It must be that to lose sight was, conversely, to die. Dead
things did not walk about. They lay down and did not move.
Therefore the thing in the wood concluded that it must be
dead, and so it lay down by the path, not far away from
Kimbo's scattered body, lay down and believed itself dead.

Alton Drew came up through the dusk to the wood. He was
frankly worried. He whistled again, and then called, and
there was still no response, and he said again, "The ol' flea-
bus never done this before," and shook his heavy head. It
was past milking time, and Cory would need him. "Kimbo!"
he roared. The cry echoed through the shadows, and Alton
flipped on the safety catch of his rifle and put the butt on
the ground beside the path. Leaning on it, he took off his
cap and scratched the back of his head, wondering. The
rifle butt sank into what he thought was soft earth; he staggered and stepped into the chest of the thing that lay beside
the path. His foot went up to the ankle in its yielding rottenness, and he swore and jumped back.

"*Whew!* Somp'n sure dead as hell there! Ugh!" He
swabbed at his boot with a handful of leaves while the monster lay in the growing blackness with the edges of the deep
footprint in its chest sliding into it, filling it up. It lay there
regarding him dimly out of its muddy eyes, thinking it was
dead because of the darkness, watching the articulation of
Alton Drew's joints, wondering at this new incautious
creature.

Alton cleaned the butt of his gun with more leaves and
went on up the path, whistling anxiously for Kimbo.

Clissa Drew stood in the door of the milk shed, very lovely in red-checked gingham and a blue apron. Her hair was clean yellow, parted in the middle and stretched tautly back to a heavy braided knot. "Cory! Alton!" she called a little sharply.

"Well?" Cory responded gruffly from the barn, where he was stripping off the Ayrshire. The dwindling streams of milk plopped pleasantly into the froth of a full pail.

"I've called and called," said Clissa. "Supper's cold, and Babe won't eat until you come. Why—where's Alton?"

Cory grunted, heaved the stool out of the way, threw over the stanchion lock and slapped the Ayrshire on the rump. The cow backed and filled like a towboat, clattered down the line and out into the barnyard. "Ain't back yet."

"Not back?" Clissa came in and stood by him as he sat by the next cow, put his forehead against the warm flank. "But, Cory, he said he'd—"

"Yeh, yeh, I know. He said he'd be back fer the milkin'. I heard him. Well, he ain't."

"And you have to— Oh, Cory, I'll help you finish up. Alton would be back if he could. Maybe he's—"

"Maybe he's treed a blue jay," snapped her husband. "Him an' that damn dog." He gestured hugely with one hand while the other went on milking. "I got twenty-six head o' cows to milk. I got pigs to feed an' chickens to put to bed. I got to toss hay for the mare and turn the team out. I got harness to mend and a wire down in the night pasture. I got wood to split an' carry." He milked for a moment in silence, chewing on his lip. Clissa stood twisting her hands together, trying to think of something to stem the tide. It wasn't the first time Alton's hunting had interfered with the chores. "So I got to go ahead with it. I can't interfere with Alton's spoorin'. Every damn time that hound o' his smells out a squirrel I go without my supper. I'm gettin' sick and—"

"Oh, I'll help you!" said Clissa. She was thinking of the spring, when Kimbo had held four hundred pounds of raging black bear at bay until Alton could put a bullet in its brain, the time Babe had found a bearcub and started to carry it home, and had fallen into a freshet, cutting her head. You can't hate a dog that has saved your child for you, she thought.

"You'll do nothin' of the kind!" Cory growled. "Get back to the house. You'll find work enough there. I'll be along when I can. Dammit, Clissa, don't cry! I didn't mean to— Oh, shucks!" He got up and put his arms around her. "I'm wrought up," he said. "Go on now. I'd no call to speak that way to you. I'm sorry. Go back to Babe. I'll put a stop to this for good tonight. I've had enough. There's work here for four farmers an' all we've got is me an' that—that huntsman. Go on now, Clissa."

"All right," she said into his shoulder. "But, Cory, hear him out first when he comes back. He might be unable to come back this time. Maybe he . . . he—"

"Ain't nothin' kin hurt my brother that a bullet will hit. He can take care of himself. He's got no excuse good enough this time. Go on, now. Make the kid eat."

Clissa went back to the house, her young face furrowed. If Cory quarreled with Alton now and drove him away, what with the drought and the creamery about to close and all, they just couldn't manage. Hiring a man was out of the question. Cory'd have to work himself to death, and he just wouldn't be able to make it. No one man could. She sighed and went into the house. It was seven o'clock, and the milking not done yet. Oh, why did Alton have to—

Babe was in bed at nine when Clissa heard Cory in the shed, slinging the wire cutters into a corner. "Alton back yet?" they both said at once as Cory stepped into the kitchen; and as she shook her head he clumped over to the stove, and lifting a lid, spat into the coals. "Come to bed," he said.

She laid down her stitching and looked at his broad back. He was twenty-eight, and he walked and acted like a man ten years older, and looked like a man five years younger. "I'll be up in a while," Clissa said.

Cory glanced at the corner behind the wood box where Alton's rifle usually stood, then made an unspellable, disgusted sound and sat down to take off his heavy muddy shoes.

"It's after nine," Clissa volunteered timidly. Cory said nothing, reaching for house slippers.

"Cory, you're not going to—"

"Not going to what?"

"Oh, nothing. I just thought that maybe Alton—"

"Alton!" Cory flared. "The dog goes hunting field mice. Alton goes hunting the dog. Now you want me to go hunting Alton. That's what you want?"

"I just— He was never this late before."

"I won't do it! Go out lookin' for him at nine o'clock in the night? I'll be damned! He has no call to use us so, Clissa."

Clissa said nothing. She went to the stove, peered into the wash boiler, set it aside at the back of the range. When she turned around, Cory had his shoes and coat on again.

"I knew you'd go," she said. Her voice smiled though she did not.

"I'll be back durned soon," said Cory. "I don't reckon he's strayed far. It is late. I ain't feared for him, but—" He broke his 12-gauge shotgun, looked through the barrels, slipped two shells into the breech and a box of them into his pocket. "Don't wait up," he said over his shoulder as he went out.

"I won't," Clissa replied to the closed door, and went back to her stitching by the lamp.

The path up the slope to the wood was very dark when Cory went up it, peering and calling. The air was chill and quiet, and a fetid odor of mold hung in it. Cory blew the taste of it out through impatient nostrils, drew it in again with the next breath, and swore. "Nonsense," he muttered. "Houn'-dawg. Huntin', at ten in th' night, too. Alton!" he bellowed. "Alton Drew!" Echoes answered him, and he entered the wood. The huddled thing he passed in the dark heard him and felt the vibrations of his footsteps and did not move because it thought it was dead.

Cory strode on, looking around and ahead and not down since his feet knew the path.

"Alton!"

"That you, Cory?"

Cory Drew froze. That corner of the wood was thickly set and as dark as a burial vault. The voice he heard was choked, quiet, penetrating.

"Alton?"

"I found Kimbo, Cory."

"Where the hell have you been?" shouted Cory furiously. He disliked this pitch-blackness; he was afraid at the tense hopelessness of Alton's voice, and he mistrusted his ability to stay angry at his brother.

"I called him, Cory. I whistled at him, an' the ol' devil didn't answer."

"I can say the same for you, you . . . you louse. Why weren't you to milkin'? Where are you? You caught in a trap?"

"The houn' never missed answerin' me before, you know," said the tight, monotonous voice from the darkness.

"Alton! What the devil's the matter with you? What do I care if your mutt didn't answer? Where—"

"I guess because he ain't never died before," said Alton, refusing to be interrupted.

"You *what?*" Cory clicked his lips together twice and then said: "Alton, you turned crazy? What's that you say?"

"Kimbo's dead."

"Kim . . . oh! Oh!" Cory was seeing that picture again in his mind—Babe sprawled unconscious in the freshet, and Kimbo raging and snapping against a monster bear, holding her back until Alton could get there. "What happened, Alton?" he asked more quietly.

"I aim to find out. Someone tore him up."

"*Tore him up?*"

"There ain't a bit of him left tacked together, Cory. Every damn joint in his body tore apart. Guts out of him."

"Good God! Bear, you reckon?"

"No bear, nor nothin' on four legs. He's all here. None of him's been et. Whoever done it just killed him an'—tore him up."

"Good God!" Cory said again. "Who could've—" There was a long silence, then: "Come 'long home," he said almost gently. "There's no call for you to set up by him all night."

"I'll set. I aim to be here at sunup, an' I'm goin' to start trackin', an' I'm goin' to keep trackin' till I find the one done this job on Kimbo."

"You're drunk or crazy, Alton."

"I ain't drunk. You can think what you like about the rest of it. I'm stickin' here."

"We got a farm back yonder. Remember? I ain't going to milk twenty-six head o' cows again in the mornin' like I did jest now, Alton."

"Somebody's got to. I can't be there. I guess you'll just have to, Cory."

"You dirty scum!" Cory screamed. "You'll come back with me now or I'll know why!"

Alton's voice was still tight, half-sleepy. "Don't you come no nearer, bud."

Cory kept moving toward Alton's voice.

"I said—" the voice was very quiet now—"*stop where you are.*" Cory kept coming. A sharp click told of the release of the .32-40's safety. Cory stopped.

"You got your gun on me, Alton?" Cory whispered.

"Thass right, bud. You ain't a'trompin' up these tracks for me. I need 'em at sunup."

A full minute passed, and the only sound in the blackness was that of Cory's pained breathing. Finally:

"I got my gun, too, Alton. Come home."

"You can't see to shoot me."

"We're even on that."

"We ain't. I know just where you stand, Cory. I been here four hours."

"My gun scatters."

"My gun kills."

Without another word Cory Drew turned on his heel and stamped back to the farm.

Black and liquescent it lay in the blackness, not alive, not understanding death, believing itself dead. Things that were alive saw and moved about. Things that were not alive could do neither. It rested its muddy gaze on the line of trees at the crest of the rise, and deep within it thoughts trickled wetly. It lay huddled, dividing its new-found facts, dissecting them as it had dissected live things when there was light, comparing, concluding, pigeonholing.

The trees at the top of the slope could just be seen, as their trunks were a fraction of a shade lighter than the dark sky behind them. At length they, too, disappeared, and for a moment sky and trees were a monotone. The thing knew it was dead now, and like many a being before it, it wondered how long it must stay like this. And then the sky beyond the trees grew a little lighter. That was a manifestly impossible occurrence, thought the thing, but it could see it and it must be so. Did dead things live again? That was curious. What about dismembered dead things? It would wait and see.

The sun came hand over hand up a beam of light. A bird somewhere made a high yawning peep, and as an owl killed a shrew, a skunk pounced on another, so that the night shift deaths and those of the day could go on without cessation. Two flowers nodded archly to each other, comparing their pretty clothes. A dragon fly nymph decided it was tired of looking serious and cracked its back open, to crawl out and dry gauzily. The first golden ray sheared down between the trees, through the grasses, passed over the mass in the shadowed bushes. "I am alive again," thought the thing that could not possibly live. "I am alive, for I see clearly." It stood up on its thick legs, up into the golden glow. In a little while the wet flakes that had grown during the night dried in the sun, and when it took its first steps, they cracked off and a little shower of them fell away. It walked up the slope to find Kimbo, to see if he, too, were alive again.

Babe let the sun come into her room by opening her eyes. Uncle Alton was gone—that was the first thing that ran through her head. Dad had come home last night and had shouted at mother for an hour. Alton was plumb crazy. He'd turned a gun on his own brother. If Alton ever came ten feet into Cory's land, Cory would fill him so full of holes he'd look like a tumbleweed. Alton was lazy, shiftless, selfish, and one or two other things of questionable taste but undoubted vividness. Babe knew her father. Uncle Alton would never be safe in this county. She bounced out of bed in the enviable way of the very young, and ran to the window. Cory was trudging down to the night pasture with two bridles over his arm, to get the team. There were kitchen noises from downstairs.

Babe ducked her head in the washbowl and shook off the water like a terrier before she toweled. Trailing clean shirt and dungarees, she went to the head of the stairs, slid into the shirt, and began her morning ritual with the trousers. One step down was a step through the right leg. One more, and she was into the left. Then, bouncing step by step on both feet, buttoning one button per step, she reached the bottom fully dressed and ran into the kitchen.

"Didn't Uncle Alton come back a-tall, Mum?"

"Morning, Babe. No, dear." Clissa was too quiet, smiling too much. Babe thought shrewdly, she wasn't happy.

"Where'd he go, Mum?"

"We don't know, Babe. Sit down and eat your breakfast."

"What's a misbegotten, Mum?" the Babe asked suddenly. Her mother nearly dropped the dish she was drying. "Babe! You must never say that again!"

"Oh. Well, why is Uncle Alton, then?"

"Why is he what?"

Babe's mouth muscled around an outsize spoonful of oatmeal. "A misbe—"

"Babe!"

"All right, Mum," said Babe with her mouth full. "Well, why?"

"I told Cory not to shout last night," Clissa said half to herself.

"Well, whatever it means, he isn't," said Babe with finality. "Did he go hunting again?"

"He went to look for Kimbo, darling."

"Kimbo? Oh, Mummy, is Kimbo gone, too? Didn't he come back either?"

"No, dear. Oh, please, Babe, stop asking questions!"

"All right. Where do you think they went?"

"Into the north woods. Be quiet."

Babe gulped away at her breakfast. An idea struck her; and as she thought of it she ate slower and slower, and cast more and more glances at her mother from under the lashes of her tilted eyes. It would be awful if daddy did anything to Uncle Alton. Someone ought to warn him.

Babe was halfway to the woods when Alton's .32-40 sent echoes giggling up and down the valley.

Cory was in the south thirty, riding a cultivator and cussing at the team of grays when he heard the gun. "Hoa," he called to the horses, and sat a moment to listen to the sound. "One-two-three, four," he counted. "Saw someone, blasted away at him. Had a chance to take aim and give him another, care-ful. My God!" He threw up the cultivator points and steered the team into the shade of three oaks. He hobbled the gelding with swift tosses of a spare strap, and headed for the woods. "Alton a killer," he murmured, and doubled back to the house for his gun. Clissa was standing just outside the door.

"Get shells!" he snapped and flung into the house. Clissa followed him. He was strapping his hunting knife on before she could get a box off the shelf. "Cory—"

"Hear that gun, did you? Alton's off his nut. He don't waste lead. He shot at someone just then, and he wasn't fixin' to shoot pa'tridges when I saw him last. He was out to get a man. Gimme my gun."

"Cory, Babe—"

"You keep her here. Oh, God, this is a helluva mess. I can't stand much more." Cory ran out the door.

Clissa caught his arm: "Cory, I'm trying to tell you. Babe isn't here. I've called, and she isn't here."

Cory's heavy, young-old face tautened. "Babe— Where did you last see her?"

"Breakfast." Clissa was crying now.

"She say where she was going?"

"No. She asked a lot of questions about Alton and where he'd gone."

"Did you say?"

Clissa's eyes widened, and she nodded, biting the back of her hand.

"You shouldn't ha' done that, Clissa," he gritted, and ran toward the woods, Clissa looking after him, and in that moment she could have killed herself.

Cory ran with his head up, straining with his legs and lungs and eyes at the long path. He puffed up the slope to the woods, agonized for breath after the forty-five minutes' heavy going. He couldn't even notice the damp smell of mold in the air.

He caught a movement in a thicket to his right, and dropped. Struggling to keep his breath, he crept forward until he could see clearly. There was something there, all right. Something black, keeping still. Cory relaxed his legs and torso completely to make it easier for his heart to pump some strength back into them, and slowly raised the 12-gauge until it bore on the thing hidden in the thicket.

"Come out!" Cory said when he could speak.

Nothing happened.

"Come out or by God I'll shoot!" rasped Cory.

There was a long moment of silence, and his finger tightened on the trigger.

"You asked for it," he said, and as he fired the thing leaped sideways into the open, screaming.

It was a thin little man dressed in sepulchral black, and bearing the rosiest little baby-face Cory had ever seen. The face was twisted with fright and pain. The little man scrambled to his feet and hopped up and down saying over and over, "Oh, my hand. Don't shoot again! Oh, my hand. Don't shoot again!" He stopped after a bit, when Cory had climbed to his feet, and he regarded the farmer out of sad china-blue eyes. "You shot me," he said reproachfully, holding up a little bloody hand. "Oh, my goodness!"

Cory said, "Now, who the hell are you?"

The man immediately became hysterical, mouthing such a flood of broken sentences that Cory stepped back a pace and half-raised his gun in self-defense. It seemed to consist mostly of "I lost my papers," and "I didn't do it," and "It was horrible. Horrible. Horrible," and "The dead man," and "Oh, don't shoot again."

Cory tried twice to ask him a question, and then he stepped over and knocked the man down. He lay on the ground writhing and moaning and blubbering and putting his bloody hand to his mouth where Cory had hit him.

"Now, what's going on around here?"

The man rolled over and sat up. "I didn't do it!" he sobbed. "I didn't! I was walking along and I heard the gun and I heard some swearing and an awful scream and I went over there and peeped and I saw the dead man and I ran away and you came and I hid and you shot me and—"

"*Shut up!*" The man did, as if a switch had been thrown. "Now," said Cory, pointing along the path, "you say there's a dead man up there?"

The man nodded and began crying in earnest. Cory helped him up. "Follow this path back to my farmhouse," he said. "Tell my wife to fix up your hand. *Don't* tell her anything else. And wait there until I come. Hear?"

"Yes. Thank you. Oh, thank you. *Snff.*"

"Go on now." Cory gave him a gentle shove in the right direction and went alone, in cold fear, up the path to the spot where he had found Alton the night before.

He found him here now, too, and Kimbo. Kimbo and Alton had spent several years together in the deepest friendship; they had hunted and fought and slept together, and the lives they owed each other were finished now. They were dead together. It was terrible that they had died the same way. Cory Drew was a strong man, but he gasped and fainted dead away when he saw what the thing of the mold had done to his brother and his brother's dog.

The little man in black hurried down the path, whimpering and holding his injured hand as if he rather wished he could limp with it. After a while the whimper faded away, and the hurried stride changed to a walk as the gibbering terror of the last hour receded. He drew two deep breaths, said: "My goodness!" and felt almost normal. He bound a linen handkerchief around his wrist, but the hand kept bleeding. He tried the elbow, and that made it hurt. So he stuffed the handkerchief back in his pocket and simply waved the hand stupidly in the air until the blood clotted.

It wasn't much of a wound. Two of the balls of shot had struck him, one passing through the fleshy part of his thumb and the other scoring the side. As he thought of it, he became a little proud that he had borne a gunshot wound. He strolled along in the midmorning sunlight, feeling a dreamy communion with the boys at the front. "The whine of shot and shell—" Where had he read that? Ah, what a story this would make. "And there beside the"—what was the line—"the embattled farmer stood." Didn't the awfulest things happen in the nicest places? This was a nice forest. No screeches and snakes and deep dark menaces. Not a storybook wood at all. Shot by a gun. How exciting! He was now—he strutted—a gentleman adventurer. He did not see the great moist horror that clumped along behind him, though his nostrils crinkled a little with its foulness.

The monster had three little holes close together on its chest, and one little hole in the middle of its slimy forehead. It had three close-set pits in its back and one on the back of its head. These marks were where Alton Drew's bullets had struck and passed through. Half of the monster's shapeless face was sloughed away, and there was a deep indentation on its shoulder. This was what Alton Drew's gun butt had done after he clubbed it and struck at the thing that would not lie down after he put his four bullets through it. When these things happened the monster was not hurt or angry. It only wondered why Alton Drew acted that way. Now it followed the little man without hurrying at all, matching his stride step by step and dropping little particles of muck behind it.

The little man went on out of the wood and stood with his back against a big tree at the forest's edge, and he thought. Enough had happened to him here. What good would it do to stay and face a horrible murder inquiry, just to continue this silly, vague quest? There was supposed to be the ruin of an old, old hunting lodge deep in this wood somewhere, and perhaps it would hold the evidence he wanted. But it was a vague report—vague enough to be forgotten without regret. It would be the height of foolishness to stay for all the hicktown red tape that would follow that ghastly affair back in the wood. Ergo, it would be ridiculous to follow that farmer's advice, to go to his house and wait for him. He would go back to town.

The monster was leaning against the other side of the big tree.

The little man snuffled disgustedly at a sudden overpowering odor of rot. He reached for his handkerchief, fumbled and dropped it. As he bent to pick it up, the monster's arm *whuffed* heavily in the air where his head had been—a blow that would certainly have removed that baby-faced protuberance. The man stood up and would have put the handkerchief to his nose had it not been so bloody. The creature behind the tree lifted its arm again just as the little man tossed the handkerchief away and stepped out into the field, heading across country to the distant highway that would take him back to town. The monster pounced on the handkerchief, picked it up, studied it, tore it across several times, and inspected the tattered edges. Then it gazed vacantly at the disappearing figure of the little man, and finding him no longer interesting, turned back into the woods.

Babe broke into a trot at the sound of the shots. It was important to warn Uncle Alton about what her father had said, but it was more interesting to find out what he had bagged. Oh, he'd bagged it, all right. Uncle Alton never fired without killing. This was about the first time she had ever heard him blast away like that. Must be a bear, she thought excitedly, tripping over a root, sprawling, rolling to her feet again, without noticing the tumble. She'd love to have another bearskin in her room. Where would she put it? Maybe they could line it and she could have it for a blanket. Uncle Alton could sit on it and read to her in the evening— Oh, no. No. Not with this trouble between him and dad. Oh, if she could only do something! She tried to run faster, worried and anticipating, but she was out of breath and went more slowly instead.

At the top of the rise by the edge of the woods she stopped and looked back. Far down in the valley lay the south thirty. She scanned it carefully, looking for her father. The new furrows and the old were sharply defined, and her keen eyes saw immediately that Cory had left the line with the cultivator and had angled the team over to the shade trees without finishing his row. That wasn't like him. She could see the team now, and Cory's pale-blue denim was not in sight.

A little nearer was the house; and as her gaze fell on it she moved out of the cleared pathway. Her father was coming; she had seen his shotgun and he was running. He could really cover ground when he wanted to. He must be chasing her, she thought immediately. He'd guessed that she would run toward the sound of the shots, and he was going to follow her tracks to Uncle Alton and shoot him. She knew that he was as good a woodsman as Alton; he would most certainly see her tracks. Well, she'd fix him.

She ran along the edge of the wood, being careful to dig her heels deeply into the loam. A hundred yards of this, and she angled into the forest and ran until she reached a particularly thick grove of trees. Shinnying up like a squirrel, she squirmed from one close-set tree to another until she could go no farther back toward the path, then dropped lightly to the ground and crept on her way, now stepping very gently. It would take him an hour to beat around for her trail, she thought proudly, and by that time she could easily get to Uncle Alton. She giggled to herself as she thought of the way she had fooled her father. And the little sound of laughter drowned out, for her, the sound of Alton's hoarse dying scream.

She reached and crossed the path and slid through the brush beside it. The shots came from up around here somewhere. She stopped and listened several times, and then suddenly heard something coming toward her, fast. She ducked under cover, terrified, and a little baby-faced man in black, his blue eyes wide with horror, crashed blindly past her, the leather case he carried catching on the branches. It spun a moment and then fell right in front of her. The man never missed it.

Babe lay there for a long moment and then picked up the case and faded into the woods. Things were happening too fast for her. She wanted Uncle Alton, but she dared not call. She stopped again and strained her ears. Back toward the edge of the wood she heard her father's voice, and another's—probably the man who had dropped the briefcase. She dared not go over there. Filled with enjoyable terror, she thought hard, then snapped her fingers in triumph. She and Alton had played Injun many times up here; they had a whole repertoire of secret signals. She had practiced bird-calls until she knew them better than the birds themselves. What would it be? Ah—blue jay. She threw back her head and by some youthful alchemy produced a nerve-shattering screech that would have done justice to any jay that ever flew. She repeated it, and then twice more.

The response was immediate—the call of a blue jay, four times, spaced two and two. Babe nodded to herself happily. That was the signal that they were to meet immediately at The Place. The Place was a hide-out that he had discovered and shared with her, and not another soul knew of it; an angle of rock beside a stream not far away. It wasn't exactly a cave, but almost. Enough so to be entrancing. Babe trotted happily away toward the brook. She had just known that Uncle Alton would remember the call of the blue jay, and what it meant.

In the tree that arched over Alton's scattered body

perched a large jay bird, preening itself and shining in the sun. Quite unconscious of the presence of death, hardly noticing the Babe's realistic cry, it screamed again four times, two and two.

It took Cory more than a moment to recover himself from what he had seen. He turned away from it and leaned weakly against a pine, panting. Alton. That was Alton lying there, in—parts.

"God! God, God, God—"

Gradually his strength returned, and he forced himself to turn again. Stepping carefully, he bent and picked up the .32-40. Its barrel was bright and clean, but the butt and stock were smeared with some kind of stinking rottenness. Where had he seen the stuff before? Somewhere—no matter. He cleaned it off absently, throwing the befouled bandanna away afterward. Through his mind ran Alton's words—was that only last night?—*"I'm goin' to start trackin'. An' I'm goin' to keep trackin' till I find the one done this job on Kimbo."*

Cory searched shrinkingly until he found Alton's box of shells. The box was wet and sticky. That made it—better, somehow. A bullet wet with Alton's blood was the right thing to use. He went away a short distance, circled around till he found heavy footprints, then came back.

"I'm a-trackin' for you, bud," he whispered thickly, and began. Through the brush he followed its wavering spoor, amazed at the amount of filthy mold about, gradually associating it with the thing that had killed his brother. There was nothing in the world for him any more but hate and doggedness. Cursing himself for not getting Alton home last night, he followed the tracks to the edge of the woods. They led him to a big tree there, and there he saw something else —the footprints of the little city man. Nearby lay some tattered scraps of linen, and—what was that?

Another set of prints—small ones. Small, stub-toed ones. Babe's.

"Babe!" Cory screamed. "Babe!"

No answer. The wind sighed. Somewhere a blue jay called.

Babe stopped and turned when she heard her father's voice, faint with distance, piercing.

"Listen at him holler," she crooned delightedly. "Gee, he sounds mad." She sent a jay bird's call disrespectfully back to him and hurried to The Place.

It consisted of a mammoth boulder beside the brook. Some upheaval in the glacial age had cleft it, cutting out a huge, V-shaped chunk. The widest part of the cleft was at the water's edge, and the narrowest was hidden by bushes. It made a little ceilingless room, rough and uneven and full of potholes and cavelets inside, and yet with quite a level floor.

Babe parted the bushes and peered down the cleft.

"Uncle Alton!" she called softly. There was no answer. Oh, well, he'd be along. She scrambled in and slid down to the floor.

She loved it here. It was shaded and cool, and the chattering little stream filled it with shifting golden lights and laughing gurgles. She called again, on principle, and then perched on an outcropping to wait. It was only then she realized that she still carried the little man's briefcase.

She turned it over a couple of times and then opened it. It was divided in the middle by a leather wall. On one side were a few papers in a large yellow envelope, and on the other some sandwiches, a candy bar, and an apple. With a youngster's complacent acceptance of manna from heaven, Babe fell to. She saved one sandwich for Alton, mainly because she didn't like its highly spiced bologna. The rest made quite a feast.

She was a little worried when Alton hadn't arrived, even after she had consumed the apple core. She got up and tried to skim some flat pebbles across the roiling brook, and she stood on her hands, and she tried to think of a story to tell herself, and she tried just waiting. Finally, in desperation, she turned again to the briefcase, took out the papers, curled up by the rocky wall and began to read them. It was something to do, anyway.

There was an old newspaper clipping that told about strange wills that people had left. An old lady had once left a lot of money to whoever would make the trip from the Earth to the Moon and back. Another had financed a home for cats whose masters and mistresses had died. A man left thousands of dollars to the first man who could solve a certain mathematical problem and prove his solution. But one item was blue-penciled. It was:

One of the strangest of wills still in force is that of Thaddeus M. Kirk, who died in 1920. It appears that he built an elaborate mausoleum with burial vaults for all the remains of his family. He collected and removed caskets from all over the country to fill the designated niches. Kirk was the last of his line; there were no relatives when he died. His will stated that the mausoleum was to be kept in repair permanently, and that a certain sum was to be set aside as a reward for whoever could produce the body of his grandfather, Roger Kirk, whose niche is still empty. Anyone finding this body is eligible to receive a substantial fortune.

Babe yawned vaguely over this, but kept on reading because there was nothing else to do. Next was a thick sheet of business correspondence, bearing the letterhead of a firm of lawyers. The body of it ran:

> In regard to your query regarding the will of Thaddeus Kirk, we are authorized to state that his grandfather was a man about five feet, five inches, whose left arm had been broken and who had a triangular silver plate set into his skull. There is no information as to the whereabouts of his death. He disappeared and was declared legally dead after the lapse of fourteen years.
>
> The amount of the reward as stated in the will, plus accrued interest, now amounts to a fraction over sixty-two thousand dollars. This will be paid to anyone who produces the remains, providing that said remains answer descriptions kept in our private files.

There was more, but Babe was bored. She went on to the little black notebook. There was nothing in it but penciled and highly abbreviated records of visits to libraries; quotations from books with titles like "History of Angelina and Tyler Counties" and "Kirk Family History." Babe threw that aside, too. Where could Uncle Alton be?

She began to sing tunelessly, "Tumalumalum tum, ta ta ta," pretending to dance a minuet with flowing skirts like a girl she had seen in the movies. A rustle of the bushes at the entrance to The Place stopped her. She peeped upward, saw them being thrust aside. Quickly she ran to a tiny cul-de-sac in the rock wall, just big enough for her to hide in. She giggled at the thought of how surprised Uncle Alton would be when she jumped out at him.

She heard the newcomer come shuffling down the steep slope of the crevice and land heavily on the floor. There was something about the sound— What was it? It occurred to her that though it was a hard job for a big man like Uncle Alton to get through the little opening in the bushes, she could hear no heavy breathing. She heard no breathing at all!

Babe peeped out into the main cave and squealed in utmost horror. Standing there was, not Uncle Alton, but a massive caricature of a man: a huge thing like an irregular mud doll, clumsily made. It quivered and parts of it glistened and parts of it were dried and crumby. Half of the lower left part of its face was gone, giving it a lopsided look. It had no perceptible mouth or nose, and its eyes were crooked, one higher than the other, both a dingy brown with no whites at all. It stood quite still looking at her, its only movement a steady unalive quivering of its body.

It wondered about the queer little noise Babe had made.

Babe crept far back against a little pocket of stone, her brain running round and round in tiny circles of agony. She opened her mouth to cry out, and could not. Her eyes bulged and her face flamed with the strangling effort, and the two golden ropes of her braided hair twitched and twitched as she hunted hopelessly for a way out. If only she were out in the open—or in the wedge-shaped half-cave where the thing was—or home in bed!

The thing clumped toward her, expressionless, moving

with a slow inevitability that was the sheer crux of horror. Babe lay wide-eyed and frozen, the mounting pressure of terror stilling her lungs, making her heart shake the whole world. The monster came to the mouth of the little pocket, tried to walk to her and was stopped by the sides. It was such a narrow little fissure; and it was all Babe could do to get in. The thing from the wood stood straining against the rock at its shoulders, pressing harder and harder to get to Babe. She sat up slowly, so near to the thing that its odor was almost thick enough to see, and a wild hope burst through her voiceless fear. It couldn't get in! It couldn't get in because it was too big!

The substance of its feet spread slowly under the tremendous strain, and at its shoulder appeared a slight crack. It widened as the monster unfeelingly crushed itself against the rock, and suddenly a large piece of the shoulder came away and the being twisted slushily three feet farther in. It lay quietly with its muddy eyes fixed on her, and then brought one thick arm up over its head and reached.

Babe scrambled in the inch farther she had believed impossible, and the filthy clubbed hand stroked down her back, leaving a trail of muck on the blue denim of the shirt she wore. The monster surged suddenly and, lying full length now, gained that last precious inch. A black hand seized one of her braids, and for Babe the lights went out.

When she came to, she was dangling by her hair from that same crusted paw. The thing held her high, so that her face and its featureless head were not more than a foot apart. It gazed at her with a mild curiosity in its eyes, and it swung her slowly back and forth. The agony of her pulled hair did what fear could not do—gave her a voice. She screamed. She opened her mouth and puffed up her powerful young lungs, and she sounded off. She held her throat in the position of the first scream, and her chest labored and pumped more air through the frozen throat. Shrill and monotonous and infinitely piercing, her screams.

The thing did not mind. It held her as she was, and watched. When it had learned all it could from this phenomenon, it dropped her jarringly, and looked around the half-cave, ignoring the stunned and huddled Babe. It reached over and picked up the leather briefcase and tore it twice across as if it were tissue. It saw the sandwich Babe had left, picked it up, crushed it, dropped it.

Babe opened her eyes, saw that she was free, and just as the thing turned back to her she dove between its legs and out into the shallow pool in front of the rock, paddled across and hit the other bank screaming. A vicious little light of fury burned in her; she picked up a grapefruit-sized stone and hurled it with all her frenzied might. It flew low and fast, and struck squashily on the monster's ankle. The thing was just taking a step toward the water; the stone caught it off balance, and its unpracticed equilibrium could not save it. It tottered for a long, silent moment at the edge and then splashed into the stream. Without a second look Babe ran shrieking away.

Cory Drew was following the little gobs of mold that somehow indicated the path of the murderer, and he was nearby when he first heard her scream. He broke into a run, dropping his shotgun and holding the .32-40 ready to fire. He ran with such deadly panic in his heart that he ran right past the huge cleft rock and was a hundred yards past it before she burst out through the pool and ran up the bank. He

had to run hard and fast to catch her, because anything behind her was that faceless horror in the cave, and she was
living for the one idea of getting away from there. He caught
her in his arms and swung her to him, and she screamed on
and on and on.

Babe didn't see Cory at all, even when he held her and
quieted her.

The monster lay in the water. It neither liked nor disliked
this new element. It rested on the bottom, its massive head a
foot beneath the surface, and it curiously considered the
facts that it had garnered. There was the little humming
noise of Babe's voice that sent the monster questing into the
cave. There was the black material of the briefcase that resisted so much more than green things when he tore it. There
was the little two-legged one who sang and brought him
near, and who screamed when he came. There was this new
cold moving thing he had fallen into. It was washing his body
away. That had never happened before. That was interesting.
The monster decided to stay and observe this new thing. It
felt no urge to save itself; it could only be curious.

The brook came laughing down out of its spring, ran
down from its source beckoning to the sunbeams and em-
bracing freshets and helpful brooklets. It shouted and
played with streaming little roots, and nudged the minnows
and pollywogs about in its tiny backwaters. It was a happy
brook. When it came to the pool by the cloven rock it found
the monster there, and plucked at it. It soaked the foul substances and smoothed and melted the molds, and the waters
below the thing eddied darkly with its diluted matter. It
was a thorough brook. It washed all it touched, persistently.

Where it found filth, it removed filth; and if there were layer on layer of foulness, then layer by foul layer it was removed. It was a good brook. It did not mind the poison of the monster, but took it up and thinned it and spread it in little rings round rocks downstream, and let it drift to the rootlets of water plants, that they might grow greener and lovelier. And the monster melted.

"I am smaller," the thing thought. "That is interesting. I could not move now. And now this part of me which thinks is going, too. It will stop in just a moment, and drift away with the rest of the body. It will stop thinking and I will stop being, and that, too, is a very interesting thing."

So the monster melted and dirtied the water, and the water was clean again, washing and washing the skeleton that the monster had left. It was not very big, and there was a badly-healed knot on the left arm. The sunlight flickered on the triangular silver plate set into the pale skull, and the skeleton was very clean now. The brook laughed about it for an age.

They found the skeleton, six grim-lipped men who came to find a killer. No one had believed Babe, when she told her story days later. It had to be days later because Babe had screamed for seven hours without stopping, and had lain like a dead child for a day. No one believed her at all, because her story was all about the bad fella, and they knew that the bad fella was simply a thing that her father had made up to frighten her with. But it was through her that the skeleton was found, and so the men at the bank sent a check to the Drews for more money than they had ever dreamed about. It was old Roger Kirk, sure enough, that skeleton, though it was found five miles from where he had died and sunk into the forest floor where the hot molds builded around his skeleton and emerged—a monster.

So the Drews had a new barn and fine new livestock and they hired four men. But they didn't have Alton. And they didn't have Kimbo. And Babe screams at night and has grown very thin.

No collection of fantasy would be complete without one version of the story of the three wishes. Here is one of the shortest, a wry variant by science fiction's most urbane author, editor, and critic.

Anthony Boucher

NELLTHU

Ailsa had been easily the homeliest and the least talented girl in the University, if also the most logical and level-headed. Now, almost twenty-five years later, she was the most attractive woman Martin had ever seen and, to judge from their surroundings, by some lengths the richest.

". . . so lucky running into you again after all these years," she was saying, in that indescribably aphrodisiac voice. "You know about publishers, and you can advise me on this novel. I was getting so tired of the piano . . ."

Martin had heard her piano recordings and knew they were superb—as the vocal recordings had been before them and the non-representational paintings before *them* and the fashion designs and that astonishing paper on prime numbers. He also knew that the income from all these together could hardly have furnished the Silver Room in which they dined or the Gold Room in which he later read the novel (which was of course superb) or the room whose color he never noticed because he did not sleep alone (and the word *superb* is inadequate).

There was only one answer, and Martin was gratified to observe that the coffee-bringing servant cast no shadow in the morning sun. While Ailsa still slept (superbly), Martin said, "So you're a demon."

"Naturally, sir," the unshadowed servant said, his eyes adoringly upon the sleeper. "Nellthu, at your service."

"But such service! I can imagine Ailsa-that-was working out a good spell and even wishing logically. But I thought you fellows were limited in what you could grant."

"We are, sir. Three wishes."

"But she has wealth, beauty, youth, fame, a remarkable variety of talents—all on three wishes?"

"On one, sir. Oh, I foxed her prettily on the first two." Nellthu smiled reminiscently. " *'Beauty'*—but she didn't specify, and I made her the most beautiful centenarian in the world. *'Wealth beyond the dreams of avarice'*—and of course nothing is beyond such dreams, and nothing she got. Ah, I was in form that day, sir! But the third wish . . ."

"Don't tell me she tried the old *'For my third wish I want three more wishes'!* I thought that was illegal."

"It is, sir. The paradoxes involved go beyond even our powers. No, sir," said Nellthu, with a sort of rueful admiration, "her third wish was stronger than that. She said: *'I wish that you fall permanently and unselfishly in love with me.'* "

"She was always logical," Martin admitted. "So for your own sake you had to make her beautiful and . . . adept, and since then you have been compelled to gratify her every——" He broke off and looked from the bed to the demon. "How lucky for me that she included 'unselfishly'!"

"Yes, sir," said Nellthu.

The whole idea of categorizing fiction as "fantasy" or "realism" breaks down when you examine the following story closely. The hospital background is realistic enough; only the tone of the narration gives it an odd feeling, and even that is "realism," if you like—reality, to a man waiting to die in a TB ward, is not precisely the waking reality most of us know.

What makes this story fantasy, obviously, is the hallucinatory figure of Casey. But it happens that this part of the story is not even an invention; it is drawn from the personal experience of a famous experimental hypnotist, George H. Estabrooks, who wrote about it in a book called *Hypnotism*.

Categories are useful as long as we do not chop things to fit them. Every work of art is a thing in itself; its materials have been transformed, and their source no longer matters. And all fiction is "fantasy," to one degree or another. Read this one, then, just as a story—never mind about labels.

Richard McKenna

CASEY
AGONISTES

You can't just plain die. You got to do it by the book.

That's how come I'm here in this TB ward with nine other recruits. Basic training to die.

You do it by stages. First a big ward, you walk around and go out and they call you mister. Then, if you got what it takes, a promotion to this isolation ward and they call you charles. You can't go nowhere, you meet the masks, and you get the feel of being dead.

Being dead is being weak and walled off. You hear car noises and see little doll-people down on the sidewalks, but when they come to visit you, they wear white masks and nightgowns and talk past you in the wrong voices. They're scared you'll rub some off on them. You would, too, if you knew how.

Nobody ever visits me. I had practice being dead before I come here. Maybe that's how I got to be charles so quick.

It's easy, playing dead here. You eat your pills, make out to sleep in the quiet hours and drink your milk like a good little charles. You grin at their phony joshing about how healthy you look and feel. You all know better, but them's the rules.

Sick call is when they really make you know it. It's a parade—the head doctor and nurse, the floor nurse Mary Howard and two interns, all in masks and nightgowns.

Mary pushes the wheeled rack with our fever charts on it. The doc is a tall skinhead with wooden eyes and pinchnose glasses. The head nurse is fat, with little pig eyes and a deep voice.

The doc can't see, hear, smell or touch you. He looks at your reflection in the chart and talks about you like you was real, but it's Mary that pulls down the cover and opens your pajama coat, and the interns poke and look and listen and tell the doc what they see and hear. He asks them questions for you to answer. You tell them how good you feel and they tell him.

He ain't supposed to get contaminated.

Mary's small, dark and sweet and the head nurse gives her a bad time. One intern is small and dark like Mary, with soft black eyes and very gentle. The other one is pink and chubby.

The doc's voice is high and thin, like he ain't all there below decks. The head nurse snaps at Mary, snips at the interns, and puts a kind of dog wiggle in her voice when she talks to the doc.

I'm glad not to know what's under any of their masks, except maybe Mary's, because I can likely imagine better faces for them than God did.

The head nurse makes rounds, riding the book. When she catches us out of line, like smoking or being up in a quiet hour, she gives Mary hell.

She gives us hell, too, like we was babies. She kind of hints that if we ain't respectful to her and obey her rules maybe she won't let us die after all.

Christ, how I hate that hag! I hope I meet her in hell.

That's how it struck me, first day or two in isolation. I'd

looked around for old shipmates, like a guy does, but didn't
see any. On the third day one recognized me. I thought I
knew that gravel voice, but even after he told me I couldn't
hardly believe it was old Slop Chute Hewitt.

He was skin and bones and his blue eyes had a kind of
puzzled look like I saw in them once years ago when a big
Limey sucker punched him in Nagasaki Joe's. When I remembered that, it made me know, all right.

He said glad to see me there and we both laughed. Some
of the others shuffled over in striped bathrobes and all of a
sudden I was in like Flynn, knowing Slop Chute. I found
out they called the head doc Uncle Death. The fat nurse was
Mama Death. The blond intern was Pink Waldo, the
dark one Curly Waldo, and Mary was Mary. Knowing
things like that is a kind of password.

They said Curly Waldo was sweet on Mary, but he was a
poor Italian. Pink Waldo come of good family and was trying to beat him out. They were pulling for Curly Waldo.

When they left, Slop Chute and me talked over old times
in China. I kept seeing him like he was on the *John D. Ed-
wards,* sitting with a cup of coffee topside by the after fire-
room hatch, while his snipes turned to down below. He wore
bleached dungarees and shined shoes and he looked like a
lord of the earth. His broad face and big belly. The way he
stoked chow into himself in the guinea pullman—that's what
give him his name. The way he took aboard beer and samshu
in the Kongmoon Happiness Garden. The way he swung the
little ne-sans dancing in the hotels on Skibby Hill. Now . . .
Godalmighty! It made me know.

But he still had the big jack lantern grin.

"Remember little Connie that danced at the Palais?" he asked.

I remember her, half Portygee, cute as hell.

"You know, Charley, now I'm headed for scrap, the onliest one damn thing I'm sorry for is I didn't shack with her when I had the chance."

"She was nice," I said.

"She was green fire in the velvet, Charley. I had her a few times when I was on the *Monocacy*. She wanted to shack and I wouldn't never do it. Christ, Christ, I wish I did, now!"

"I ain't sorry for anything, that I can think of."

"You'll come to it, sailor. For every guy there's some one thing. Remember how Connie used to put her finger on her nose like a Jap girl?"

"Now, Mr. Noble, you mustn't keep arthur awake in quiet hour. Lie down yourself, please."

It was Mama Death, sneaked up on us.

"Now rest like a good boy, charles, and we'll have you home before you know it," she told me on her way out.

I thought a thought at her.

The ward had green-gray linoleum, high, narrow windows, a spar-color overhead, and five bunks on a side. My bunk was at one end next to the solarium. Slop Chute was across from me in the middle. Six of us was sailors, three soldiers, and there was one marine.

We got mucho sack time, training for the long sleep. The marine bunked next to me and I saw a lot of him.

He was a strange guy. Name of Carnahan, with a pointed nose and a short upper lip and a go-to-hell stare. He most always wore his radio earphones and he was all the time grinning and chuckling like he was in a private world from the rest of us.

It wasn't the program that made him grin, either, like I thought first. He'd do it even if some housewife was yapping about how to didify the dumplings. He carried on worst during sick call. Sometimes Uncle Death looked across almost like he could hear it direct.

I asked him about it and he put me off, but finally he told me. Seems he could hypnotize himself to see a big ape and then make the ape clown around. He told me I might could get to see it too. I wanted to try, so we did.

"He's there," Carnahan would say. "Sag your eyes, look out the corners. He won't be plain at first.

"Just *expect* him, he'll come. Don't want him to do anything. You just *feel*. He'll do what's natural," he kept telling me.

I got where I could see the ape—Casey, Carnahan called him—in flashes. Then one day Mama Death was chewing out Mary and I saw him plain. He come up behind Mama and—I busted right out laughing.

He looked like a bowlegged man in an ape suit covered with red-brown hair. He grinned and made faces with a mouth full of big yellow teeth and he was furnished like John Keeno himself. I roared.

"Put on your phones so you'll have an excuse for laughing," Carnahan whispered. "Only you and me can see him, you know."

Fixing to be dead you're ready for God knows what, but Casey was sure something.

"Hell no, he ain't real," Carnahan said. "We ain't so real ourselves any more. That's why we can see him."

Carnahan told me okay to try and let Slop Chute in on it. It ended we cut the whole gang in, going slow so the masks wouldn't get suspicious.

It bothered Casey at first, us all looking at him. It was like we all had a string on him and he didn't know who to mind. He backed and filled and tacked and yawed all over the ward not able to steer himself. Only when Mama Death was there and Casey went after her, then it was like all the strings pulled the same way.

The more we watched him the plainer and stronger he got till finally he started being his own man. He came and went as he pleased and we never knew what he'd do next except that there'd be a laugh in it. Casey got more and more there for us, but he never made a sound.

He made a big difference. We all wore our earphones and giggled like idiots. Slop Chute wore his big sideways grin more often. Old Webster almost stopped griping.

There was a man filling in for a padre came to visitate us every week. Casey would sit on his knee and wiggle and drool, with one finger between those strong, yellow teeth. The man said the radio was a Godsend to us patient spirits in our hour of trial. He stopped coming.

Casey made a real show out of sick call. He kissed Mama Death smack on her mask, danced with her and bit her on the rump. He rode piggy back on Uncle Death. He even took a hand in Mary's romance.

One Waldo always went in on each side of a bunk to look, listen and feel for Uncle. Mary could go on either side. We kept count of whose side she picked and how close she stood to him. That's how we figured Pink Waldo was ahead.

Well, Casey started to shoo her gently in by Curly Waldo and then crowd her closer to him. And, you know, the count began to change in Curly's favor. Casey had something.

If no masks were around to bedevil, Casey would dance and turn handsprings. He made us all feel good.

Uncle Death smelled a rat and had the radio turned off during sick call and quiet hours. But he couldn't cut off Casey.

Something went wrong with Roby, the cheerful black boy next to Slop Chute. The masks were all upset about it and finally Mary come told him on the sly. He wasn't going to make it. They were going to flunk him back to the big ward and maybe back to the world.

Mary's good that way. We never see her face, of course, but I always imagine for her a mouth like Venus has, in that picture you see her standing in the shell.

When Roby had to go, he come around to each bunk and said goodbye. Casey stayed right behind him with his tongue stuck out. Roby kept looking around for Casey, but of course he couldn't see him.

He turned around, just before he left the ward, and all of a sudden Casey was back in the middle and scowling at him. Roby stood looking at Casey with the saddest face I ever saw him wear. Then Casey grinned and waved a hand. Roby grinned back and tears run down his black face. He waved and shoved off.

Casey took to sleeping in Roby's bunk till another recruit come in.

One day two masked orderlies loaded old Webster the whiner onto a go-to-Jesus cart and wheeled him off to x-ray. They said. But later one came back and wouldn't look at us and pushed Webster's locker out and we knew. The masks had him in a quiet room for the graduation exercises.

They always done that, Slop Chute told me, so's not to hurt the morale of the guys not able to make the grade yet. Trouble was, when a guy went to x-ray on a go-to-Jesus cart he never knew till he got back whether he was going to see the gang again.

Next morning when Uncle Death fell in for sick call Casey come bouncing down the ward and hit him a haymaker plumb on the mask.

I swear the bald-headed bastard staggered. I know his glasses fell off and Pink Waldo caught them. He said something about a moment of vertigo, and made a quick job of sick call. Casey stayed right behind him and kicked his stern post every step he took.

Mary favored Curly Waldo's side that day without any help from Casey.

After that Mama Death really got ugly. She slobbered loving care all over us to keep us knowing what we was there for. We got baths and back rubs we didn't want. Quiet hour had to start on the dot and be really quiet. She was always reading Mary off in whispers, like she knew it bothered us.

Casey followed her around aping her duck waddle and poking her behind now and again. We laughed and she thought it was at her and I guess it was. So she got Uncle Death to order the routine temperatures taken rectally, which she knew we hated. We stopped laughing and she knocked off the rectal temperatures. It was a kind of un-spoken agreement. Casey give her a worse time than ever, but we saved our laughing till she was gone.

Poor Slop Chute couldn't do anything about his big, lopsided grin that was louder than a belly laugh. Mama give him a real bad time. She arthured the hell out of him.

He was coming along first rate, had another hemorrhage, and they started taking him to the clinic on a go-to-Jesus cart instead of a chair. He was supposed to use ducks and a bedpan instead of going to the head, but he saved it up and after lights out we used to help him walk to the head. That made his reflection in the chart wrong and got him in deeper with Uncle Death.

I talked to him a lot, mostly about Connie. He said he dreamed about her pretty often now.

"I figure it means I'm near ready for the deep six, Charley."

"Figure you'll see Connie then?"

"No. Just hope I won't have to go on thinking about her then. I want it to be all night in and no reveille."

"Yeah," I said. "Me, too. What ever become of Connie?"

"I heard she ate poison right after the Reds took over Shanghai. I wonder if she ever dreamed about me?"

"I bet she did, Slop Chute," I said. "She likely used to wake up screaming and she ate the poison just to get rid of you."

He put on a big grin.

"You regret something too, Charley. You find it yet?"

"Well, maybe," I said. "Once on a stormy night at sea on

the *Black Hawk* I had a chance to push King Brody over the side. I'm sorry now I didn't."

"Just come to you?"

"Hell, no, it come to me three days later when he give me a week's restriction in Tsingtao. I been sorry ever since."

"No. It'll smell you out, Charley. You wait."

Casey was shadow boxing down the middle of the ward as I shuffled back to my bunk.

It must've been spring because the days were longer. One night, right after the nurse come through, Casey and Carnahan and me helped Slop Chute walk to the head. While he was there he had another hemorrhage.

Carnahan started for help but Casey got in the way and motioned him back and we knew Slop Chute didn't want it.

We pulled Slop Chute's pajama top off and steadied him. He went on his knees in front of the bowl and the soft, bubbling cough went on for a long time. We kept flushing it. Casey opened the door and went out to keep away the nurse.

Finally it pretty well stopped. Slop Chute was too weak to stand. We cleaned him up and I put my pajama top on him, and we stood him up. If Casey hadn't took half the load, we'd'a never got him back to his bunk.

Godalmighty! I used to carry hundred-kilo sacks of cement like they was nothing.

We went back and cleaned up the head. I washed out the pajama top and draped it on the radiator. I was in a cold sweat and my face burned when I turned in.

Across the ward Casey was sitting like a statue beside Slop Chute's bunk.

Next day was Friday, because Pink Waldo made some crack about fish to Curly Waldo when they formed up for sick call. Mary moved closer to Curly Waldo and gave Pink Waldo a cold look. That was good.

Slop Chute looked waxy, and Uncle Death seemed to see it because a gleam come into his wooden eyes. Both Waldoes listened all over Slop Chute and told Uncle what they heard in their secret language. Uncle nodded, and Casey thumbed his nose at him.

No doubt about it, the ways was greased for Slop Chute. Mama Death come back soon as she could and began to loosen the chocks. She slobbered arthurs all over Slop Chute and flittered around like women do when they smell a wedding. Casey gave her extra special hell, and we all laughed right out and she hardly noticed.

That afternoon two orderly-masks come with a go-to-Jesus cart and wanted to take Slop Chute to x-ray. Casey climbed on the cart and scowled at them.

Slop Chute told 'em shove off, he wasn't going.

They got Mary and she told Slop Chute please go, it was doctor's orders.

Sorry, no, he said.

"Please, for me, Slop Chute," she begged.

She knows our right names—that's one reason we love her. But Slop Chute shook his head, and his big jaw bone stuck out.

Mary—she had to then—called Mama Death. Mama waddled in, and Casey spit in her mask.

"Now arthur, what is this, arthur, you know we want to help you get well and go home, arthur," she arthured at

Slop Chute. "Be a good boy now, arthur, and go along to the clinic."

She motioned the orderlies to pick him up anyway. Casey hit one in the mask and Slop Chute growled, "Sheer off, you bastards!"

The orderlies hesitated.

Mama's little eyes squinted and she wiggled her hands at them. "Let's not be naughty, arthur. Doctor knows best, arthur."

The orderlies looked at Slop Chute and at each other. Casey wrapped his arms and legs around Mama Death and began chewing on her neck. He seemed to mix right into her, someway, and she broke and run out of the ward.

She come right back, though, trailing Uncle Death. Casey met him at the door and beat hell out of him all the way to Slop Chute's bunk. Mama sent Mary for the chart, and Uncle Death studied Slop Chute's reflection for a minute. He looked pale and swayed a little from Casey's beating.

He turned toward Slop Chute and breathed in deep and Casey was on him again. Casey wrapped his arms and legs around him and chewed at his mask with those big yellow teeth. Casey's hair bristled and his eyes were red as the flames of hell.

Uncle Death staggered back across the ward and fetched up against Carnahan's bunk. The other masks were scared spitless, looking all around, kind of knowing.

Casey pulled away, and Uncle Death said maybe he was wrong, schedule it for tomorrow. All the masks left in a hurry except Mary. She went back to Slop Chute and took his hand.

"I'm sorry, Slop Chute," she whispered.

"Bless you, Connie," he said, and grinned. It was the last thing I ever heard him say.

Slop Chute went to sleep, and Casey sat beside his bunk. He motioned me off when I wanted to help Slop Chute to the head after lights out. I turned in and went to sleep.

I don't know what woke me. Casey was moving around fidgety-like, but of course not making a sound. I could hear the others stirring and whispering in the dark too.

Then I heard a muffled noise—the bubbling cough again, and spitting. Slop Chute was having another hemorrhage and he had his head under the blankets to hide the sound. Carnahan started to get up. Casey waved him down.

I saw a deeper shadow high in the dark over Slop Chute's bunk. It came down ever so gently and Casey would push it back up again. The muffled coughing went on.

Casey had a harder time pushing back the shadow. Finally he climbed on the bunk straddle of Slop Chute and kept a steady push against it.

The blackness came down anyway, little by little. Casey strained and shifted his footing. I could hear him grunt and hear his joints crack.

I was breathing forced draft with my heart like to pull off its bed bolts. I heard other bedsprings creaking. Somebody across from me whimpered low, but it was sure never Slop Chute that done it.

Casey went to his knees, his hands forced almost level with his head. He swung his head back and forth and I saw his lips curled back from the big teeth clenched tight together. . . . Then he had the blackness on his shoulders like the weight of the whole world.

Casey went down on hands and knees with his back arched like a bridge. Almost I thought I heard him grunt . . . and he gained a little.

Then the blackness settled heavier, and I heard Casey's tendons pull out and his bones snap. Casey and Slop Chute disappeared under the blackness, and it overflowed from there over the whole bed . . . and more . . . and it seemed to fill the whole ward.

It wasn't like going to sleep, but I don't know anything it was like.

The masks must've towed off Slop Chute's bulk in the night, because it was gone when I woke up.

So was Casey.

Casey didn't show up for sick call and I knew then how much he meant to me. With him around to fight back I didn't feel as dead as they wanted me to. Without him I felt deader than ever. I even almost liked Mama Death when she charlesed me.

Mary came on duty that morning with a diamond on her third finger and a brighter sparkle in her eye. It was a little diamond, but it was Curly Waldo's and it kind of made up for Slop Chute.

I wished Casey was there to see it. He would've danced all around her and kissed her nice, the way he often did. Casey loved Mary.

It was Saturday. I know, because Mama Death come in and told some of us we could be wheeled to a special church hooraw before breakfast next morning if we wanted. We said no thanks. But it was a hell of a Saturday without

Casey. Sharkey Brown said it for all of us—"With Casey gone, this place is like a morgue again."

Not even Carnahan could call him up.

"Sometimes I think I feel him stir, and then again I ain't sure," he said. "It beats hell where he's went to."

Going to sleep that night was as much like dying as it could be for men already dead.

Music from far off woke me up when it was just getting light. I was going to try to cork off again, when I saw Carnahan was awake.

"Casey's around somewhere," he whispered.

"Where?" I asked, looking around. "I don't see him."

"I feel him," Carnahan said. "He's around."

The others began to wake up and look around. It was like the night Casey and Slop Chute went under. Then something moved in the solarium. . . .

It was Casey.

He come in the ward slow and bashful-like, jerking his head all around, with his eyes open wide, and looking scared we was going to throw something at him. He stopped in the middle of the ward.

"Yea, Casey!" Carnahan said in a low, clear voice.

Casey looked at him sharp.

"Yea, Casey!" we all said. "Come aboard, you hairy old bastard!"

Casey shook hands with himself over his head and went into his dance. He grinned . . . and I swear to God it was Slop Chute's big, lopsided grin he had on.

For the first time in my whole damn life I wanted to cry.

Like "Trouble with Water," this next one is just for fun; you are not expected to take the basic premise seriously, only to swallow it and enjoy what happens next. The pattern of the story is one in which science fiction excels—a wish-fulfillment fantasy, examined in sober detail to see where the catch is. And there always is a catch.

T. L. Sherred

EYE FOR
INIQUITY

We were both surprised the first time I made a ten-dollar bill. My wife sat there and her eyes were as wide as mine. We sat awhile, just looking at it. Finally she reached over to my side of the table and poked at it a little gingerly before she picked it up.

"It looks just like a real one," she said thoughtfully; "looks good, feels good. Wonder if it *is* any good."

I told her I didn't know. "Let me see it once," and she handed it over to me.

I rubbed it gently between my fingers and held it up to the light. The little whorls, so delicately traced on a geometric lathe, were clear and clean; the features of Alexander Hamilton were sharp, the eyes grimly facing to the west. The paper was reasonably crisp, the numbers solidly stamped.

I couldn't see a single thing wrong with it.

My wife is more practical than I. She said, "Maybe you can't see anything wrong with it yourself. But I want to know if they'll take it at the supermarket. We need butter."

They took the ten-dollar bill at the supermarket; we got two pounds of butter, some coffee and some meat, and I bought some magazines with the change. We went home to think it over and chased the kids outside so we could talk without interruption.

Jean looked at me. "Now what?"

I shrugged. "So we make some more ten-dollar bills. You trying to tell me we don't need any more?"

She knew better than that. "Talk sense, Mike McNally. That ten-dollar bill means that we'll have meat tomorrow instead of macaroni. But that doesn't answer my question: now what?"

I told her I wanted to think it over.

"No, you don't. Any thinking is going to be done on a corporate basis." She meant it. "If you're going ahead with this—well, I'm in it, too."

"Fair enough," I told her. "Let's wait until the kids get to bed and we'll get it straightened out. In the meantime get that other bill out again. I need a new battery, and the right front tire isn't going to last much longer."

She agreed that was fair, and took the other bill—and, I'll say right here that it was the *only* bill we had left, with pay-day three days away—out of her purse. She laid it on the coffee table in front of me, smoothing out the creases.

"All right," she said. "Go ahead."

I shifted the ten-dollar bill a little closer to me, leaned my elbows on the table, and concentrated.

Almost immediately the duplicate began to take shape; first in outline, then in color, then in fine lines of script and curlycued detail. It took about five seconds in all, I suppose. We hadn't as yet attempted to time it.

While Jean carefully examined the duplicate, I made two more, three in all besides the original. I gave Jean back the original and one of the duplicates to boot and went down to price new batteries. It was a warm day, so I piled the kids into the car and took them along with me for the ride.

After the kids get to bed and after the dishes are washed and left to dry on the sink, the house is quiet. Too quiet, sometimes, when I think how fast little children grow up and leave home. But that's a long time away, especially for the little guy. Jean brought in the beer, and we turned on the Canadian station that doesn't have commercials. They were playing Victor Herbert.

"Well?" Jean, I could tell, was a little nervous. She'd had all day to think things over with the children not underfoot. "I see they took them, all right."

"They" and "them" were the bills and the people that had sold me the tire and the battery. "Sure," I said. "Nothing to it."

Jean put down her beer and looked me straight in the eye.

"Mike, what you're doing is against the law. Do you want to go to jail, and do you want the kids to know their father—"

I stopped her right there. "You show me," I challenged her, "where what I'm doing is against the law."

"Well—"

I didn't let her get started. "In the first place, those bills are not counterfeits. They're just as real as though they were made right in Washington. They're not copies, because 'copy' implies that in some way they attempt to emulate the original. And these don't emulate anything—they're real! Just as real as could be—I showed you that on the microscope and you agreed to that."

I was right, and she knew it. I was perfectly confident that even the atoms in the original bill and the duplicates were identical.

I had her there. She just sat and looked at me, with her cigarette burning away in the ashtray. I turned up the radio a little louder. Neither of us said anything for a while.

Then she asked, "Mike, was anyone else in your family ever able to do this, anyone that you know for sure?"

I didn't think so. "My grandmother was always having some presentiments about things that came true about half the time, and my mother was always able to find things that were lost. My Aunt Mary is still having the wild and woolly dreams she's had all her life, but that's as far as it goes, if you except the fact that my own mother was born with a caul and when I was real small, before she died, she always used to insist that I would learn to make money just when I needed it most."

Jean said, "What about that relative of yours that was burned alive in Belfast?"

I was insulted. "That was County Monaghan, which is a long way from Ulster. And it was my great-grandaunt Brigid-Nora. And she was burned because her father was Spanish and because she always had plenty of gold and food during the Great Famine; not because she was a witch."

"Your grandmother always used to say she was a witch."

"Logical way to reason," I said. "Brigid-Nora was from the Connaught side of the family. You know, like the Walloons and the Flemings, or the Prussians and the Bavarians."

"Never mind your Irish history. You said your mother—"

"Yes, she said I'd have plenty of money just when I needed it most. But you're a mother yourself; you know how mothers feel about their offspring."

Jean sighed, and split the last bottle evenly between our glasses. "Your mother certainly knew her little boy. 'Just

when you need it most!' Mike, if this doesn't work out I'm
going to go back to work. I can't stand this—this no-meat,
no-clothes, no-nothing diet any more. I can't take this sort
of life much longer!"

I knew that. I couldn't take it much longer myself. Bor-
rowing five here, ten there, driving a car that hadn't been
in corporate existence for twelve years, getting gas and oil
on a pay-you-Friday basis, wearing suits that—well, you
know what I mean. I didn't like it. And the two kids would
wait a long time before they got to live in a house their
father could buy on a foreman's pay.

Regardless of what they say in comic strips, I really pro-
posed in the rumble seat of a Whippet roadster; otherwise,
I hadn't been on my knees in front of anyone since I was a
boy. But that night I just got down on the floor in front of
Jean and we really had it out; all the things that people
usually don't say, but think. I told her what I wanted and
she told me what she wanted and we both made sloppy
spectacles of ourselves. Finally we got up and went to bed.

The next morning I was up before the kids, which, for me, is
exceptional. The first thing I did after breakfast was to call
up my boss and tell him what he could do with his job. An
hour after that *his* boss called me up and hinted that all
would be forgiven if I reported for work on the afternoon
shift as usual. I hinted right back for a raise and waited until
he agreed. Then I told him what he could do with his job.

We sat out in the kitchen for almost an hour that morning
making duplicate ten-dollar bills, with Jean keeping track
until we got up to two thousand dollars in cold, hard, green
cash—more money than we had ever had at one time in our

whole married or single life. Then we dressed the kids and took a cab downtown. Shopping. Shopping for cash, with no looks at the price tags. Oh, Jean tried to sneak a look every once in a while, when she thought I didn't see, but I always ripped the tag off and stuck it in my pocket.

The bicycle and the scooter and the bigger things we had delivered; the rest we carried. The landlord's wife was immensely surprised when we came back home in another cab with the trunk full of packages; she wanted to express her sympathy over the sudden event that had caused us to go away in one taxi and return in another. Nothing serious, she hoped. We said no, it wasn't serious, and shut the door.

Well, that was the beginning. Two or three days of steady buying will buy an awful lot of clothes. In three weeks we had all we could wear and were thinking seriously of buying some things for the house. The stove we had was on its last legs before we bought it, and the furniture was all scratched and marred from when the kids were still crawling and spilling things.

But we didn't want to buy any furniture until we could find a place to live out in the country, and all the places we looked at in our Sunday drives were either too much or too far or too something. So I called Art's Bar, where I hang out sometimes on paynights.

"Art," I asked, "do you remember that real estate man that wanted to sell me that cottage before he found out I didn't have the money?"

Sure, he remembered. "As a matter of fact, he's here right now trying to sell me some insurance. Why?"

I told him I might want to see him about a new house.

"Then come on down and get him out of my hair. I need

more insurance like I need more rocks in my head. You coming down here or do you want me to send—"

No, I'd come down there. I didn't want anyone except relatives to see the crummy place where I lived. Even relatives like to rub it in.

The real estate man—even if his name was important, I couldn't remember it now—had gone over to DeBaeker's grocery for bread. He'd be right back, Art said.

All right. I could wait. I asked Art for a short beer, and he slid it deftly down to my favorite corner. It tasted a little too cold, and I warmed it a bit with my hands. This mechanical refrigeration is all right when business is rushing, but when business is slow the beer in the coils gets too cold for my taste.

"Art," I said, "the paper isn't here yet. What have you to read besides the *Neighborhood Shopper?*"

Art looked up from the cash-register tape. "I don't know, Mike. There's a whole bunch of mail I opened that I haven't had a chance to look at yet. There might be the last *Bar News* in there. Take a look for yourself while I see how much dough the night man was off last night."

He shoved over the morning mail. I used to help out Art every once in a while to make myself a few extra dollars, and he knew there wasn't anything in the mail besides the usual advertising circulars, which he had no objection to my reading.

There was no *Bar News* there, and I idly turned over the pile, glancing at advertising puffs for spigots and coil cleaners and sham glasses. Then I saw it, and looked closer. I might add that I read everything, from streetcar transfers to medicine labels to the Men Wanted posters in the post office.

This particular circular was a copy of others that every small businessman gets from his post office or Federal Reserve District. This one was just like all the rest, with warnings of flaws or errors or careless workmanship in the usual number of counterfeit bills always in circulation. This warning caught me where it hurt.

It said:

WATCH FOR THIS TEN-DOLLAR BILL
Federal Reserve Note, Series G, serial number G 6943-7088 D. Series 1934 D, with 7 printed four lower corners on obverse of bill. Portrait of Alexander Hamilton.
THIS IS AN EXCELLENT COUNTERFEIT!
and can be distinguished at first glance only by above serial number on face of bill. Special warning to groceries and clothing stores; all detected so far have been from these businesses. It is thought that since so few bills have been detected these bills are only samples being tested for public reception. If you see one of these bills, detain the passer on some reasonable pretext and call. . . .

and it gave the Federal Building telephone number.

That was enough for me. I crumpled up the circular and dropped it to the floor, with my ears waiting for it to explode. Art rolled up the tape and dropped it in the cash drawer. I sat there, thankful I was sitting. My knees wouldn't have held me.

Art drew himself a short beer. "Find anything good?"

I managed to take a shaky breath. Anything good? Hell, Art was never going to know just how good, or how bad, I felt.

"Art," I said, "I want another beer. Better give me something stronger with it." So I paid Art, got a shot and a beer, which I'm not used to, and sat back trying to get my breath back under control. I didn't realize how stupid I'd been until Art came back from the cash register with the duplicate ten in his hand.

"Here, Mike. You'd better take this ten back—pay me later, unless you want a lot of silver. Too early in the day for me, and the last two guys that came in had twenties. Okay?"

You bet it was okay. "Sure, Art. I know how it is." I took the ten from his outstretched fingers with a hand that quivered. "As a matter of fact, I shouldn't have given you that ten at all." You bet I shouldn't. "I've got the right change right here—" and I dumped a handful on the bar. "You better have one with me, yourself."

Art had another short beer; I finished my drink, and I went out to the car and sat in it and quietly had the male equivalent of hysterics. I made it home all right, and got through the rest of the day without saying much to my wife. And then I lay in bed half the night, thinking.

Now, I don't consider myself to be a crook, nor did I want to be one. I hadn't thought about it too much because those ten-dollar bills looked too good to me and Jean. But I had a decision to make; was I going to go ahead with this, or was I going to go back to the dog-eat-dog life I'd given myself and my family?

Money? Well, the Government prints it, sends it to the bank, and from there to the man who actually spends it. After passing through scores or hundreds of hands, each time acting as a buying or selling catalyst for the national economy, it wears out—the paper becomes worn or torn.

Then it is totaled, shipped back to Washington, and destroyed. But not all of it.

Inevitably some would be lost, burned by fire or drowned by water, or maybe even buried in unknown pits by anonymous misers to rot in useless solitude. A billion dollars in crisp green currency would issue from the Mint, to return worn and foreshortened by thousands of missing dollars. Would it be wrong to replace some of those lost units? The Government would still have to replace no more than they had originally printed; the people that spent the money would suffer no inflationary loss of their savings; industry would get full value and possibly even increased sales.

That's the way I had figured—no one would lose, and one family would benefit—mine. But now I had been proved wrong by some bank teller, by some sharp-eyed comparison of similar numbers. The innocents had lost when they had taken my duplicates, lost because all counterfeit money is automatically confiscated. Uncle Sam brooks no false images. Perhaps even some of my friends, some of my acquaintances, had lost because of me, and all because I had been stupid enough to use the same bill for all my duplicates.

The disgusted ceiling stared down at me and I made a mental note never to tell my wife. I'd solve this my own way, without getting her into it, and I went to sleep long after I had given up trying to find a way out.

When I got up the next morning, I duplicated a five-dollar bill.

It worked all right. There really wasn't any reason why I shouldn't be able to duplicate any one I wanted; it was just that the ten had been the first one I tried, and that only because it was the only one in the house. And it felt better to me to have a pocket full of tens than a pocket full of fives. I guess it would to most people.

When I made the first five, I looked through my billfold and took out all the fives I had, and made one more of each one. Then I went through Jean's purse and did the same. When I was finished, I had about a dozen copies, and about a dozen originals, and I felt rather proud of myself. I leaned back in my chair and began to figure the probability of some bank teller's noticing that the numbers of two five-dollar bills were identical, if the bills came into the bank two days or two weeks apart.

Then the handful of bills and I went out to do my shopping.

I think the best thing to do would be to tell what I did for the next few months. The first bunch of fives I got rid of in different stores, one or two in each one. Every once in a while I would be able to convert four five-dollar bills into a twenty, or into a pair of tens. Then I would duplicate the bigger bill, and spend the original and the copy in two widely separated stores.

In two or three months I was in more business places, more bars, and more odd shops than I'd been in the past ten years. But I did have one bit of trouble; it got so that the clerks would good-naturedly wail when I went into a store, and complain that I must be a millionaire, because I never seemed to have less than a five or a ten or a twenty. I didn't like the idea of having attention called to me in such a way, even though nothing but pleasant conversation came out of it. So the only thing I could do was to spend a lot of time and traveling so that I hit the same stores as seldom as possible. I had a little black book with all the addresses I'd visited, with a note in my own private code telling what I'd bought.

Every week or so I'd drop down to the bank and deposit what seemed to be a reasonable figure. And what a pleasant feeling it was to be able to walk into a bank with a bankbook and a fistful of money to put in! It was really the first time in my life that I had ever used a bank for anything else but a place to get money orders, or to cash in a savings bond that my boss had insisted I pay for with the payroll deduction plan.

It even got so the clerks in the bank would give me a big smile and say, "Business must be doing all right, Mr. McNally." I'd give them a pontifical frown and complain that the country was going to the dogs with high taxes. I knew that was what I was expected to say. Anyone who deposits every week, just as regular as clockwork, better than a hundred dollars is bound to complain about taxes. The more deposit, the louder the bellow.

And we bought a new car. Well, not exactly new, but it was only a year old. These big cars depreciate a lot the first year. The salesman who sold it to me must have thought he was pulling a fast one when he got rid of that gas-eater, but that didn't worry me any. The more gas it used, the more chances I got to get into a gas station where I could get rid of another bill. I always had wanted a big car anyway. My old car I sold to the junkman, with a twinge of regret when he hauled it away with the fenders throbbing gently in the wind.

My wife, who all this time never did find out about the mess I had almost gotten into with the original setup, had for the first time in her life all the clothes, all the household appliances, all the little luxuries she wanted. But she wanted to buy a house.

"Mike," she said, "there's a lot of houses around Twelve Mile Road. Let's get some place where the kids can play."

I told her no dice, and managed to make it stick. After all, I had just a little bit better than a down payment in the bank, and I didn't want to take any chances until I had the ability to take care of all the expenses that would be bound to arise with the purchase of a new home.

So we just stayed where we were, with the landlady's eyes popping every time we came home with something new. She tried to pump, but we don't pump very well with people we don't like.

There was one place where I had trouble, and it was the one place I didn't want it. Naturally, I couldn't stop going to Art's Bar. I had been going in there for years, and the last thing I wanted was to have someone think I was going high hat. On top of that, I enjoy playing cards, and I like to drink beer. So I dropped in there just as often as I always did, and tried to think of answers for all the questions that were shot at me. When someone who's always been on the verge of bankruptcy—and most of Art's customers are that way; it was a family bar—suddenly shows up with good clothes and a new car and the ability to buy a friend a beer once in a while, then questions are bound to arise. I told them I was doing this and doing that, and still didn't satisfy their curiosity.

Finally I called the man who'd been trying to sell me some

more insurance for years. He came out to the house and gave me one of his high-pressure sales talks. I pretended to be taking notes of his figures, but I wasn't. I was checking his sales pitch. I bought some more insurance and memorized a lot of the words and phrases he used. The next time at Art's when someone asked me what I was doing for a living I told them I was selling insurance, and went into the sales talk I'd memorized. They let me alone after that, apparently convinced.

Late in 1951 we bought our house. (We still live there, if you're curious. Drop in and see us some time, if you're ever around the Utica Road, near Rochester. It's the big one on the far corner, near the golf course.) We paid spot cash for the whole thing, on a seventy-by-two-hundred-foot lot. The kids fell in love with it at first sight, naturally, and I think it was the slide and the swings in the back yard that did it. It didn't take long before they were just as brown as Polynesians, and it didn't take long before Jean was the same. She spent—and spends—more time digging in the yard planting flowers than I do sleeping.

It was really a wonderful life. We'd get up when we felt like it—in the summer, when the kids weren't in school—and sit around until we felt like doing something. When we found something to do we did it without counting out in advance what we could afford to spend. If we wanted to stay overnight in town we did it, and we stayed at whatever hotel we wanted to. And when we registered at the hotel we didn't have to ask first how much the room was, and Jean could go right into the lobby with me without feeling self-conscious about the clothes she happened to be wearing. It amused me a little when I figured that out; before we'd had enough money we used to feel self-conscious no matter what we were wearing, no matter how well we were dressed. Now we didn't care how we looked.

Once we registered at the Statler when we came back from a little ride to Tilbury, Ontario, and Jean and I and the kids were wearing shorts. We just went to our room, had a good night's sleep, had breakfast, and were home before we even thought of how many stares we'd collected in the glittering lobby. We thought that over, analyzed it, and began to laugh.

When the kids got out of school in the summer of 1953, we went for a long trip, this time to Wisconsin Dells, and then to the Black Hills. When we got back, in the middle of August, the mailbox was full of the usual advertising, and after a cursory glance at the collection, I threw it all into the incinerator, which was a mistake. That was in August. In September we had a caller.

It was one of these Indian summer days, with the breeze and the warm sun, and the overtones of the children playing in the yard.

"My name," he said, "is Morton. Frank Morton. I'm with the Bureau of Internal Revenue."

Jean almost collapsed.

"Nice place you have here, Mr. McNally," he said. "I've always admired it."

I thanked him for that. "We like it, Mr. Morton. The kids like it here away from the traffic." I couldn't think of anything else to say.

He agreed. "As a matter of fact, my boy comes over to play here quite often."

I was surprised at that.

"You must have seen him," Morton went on. "Fat little fellow!"

I knew who he meant. "Little Frankie? Why, sure! He likes my wife's cookies. Doesn't he, Jean?"

Jean said that reminded her of what she had in the oven, and excused herself to let me face the music alone. I didn't mind; I'd always told her that all this was my idea, and I'd take care of whatever happened. I knew she'd be right out in the kitchen with her ear right up against the door.

"That isn't what I was after, Mr. McNally. This is just what you might call a friendly call, in a way."

I liked that. "Always glad to have you, Mr. Morton. You must live in that house across from the grocery store."

Yes, he did. "I say a 'friendly call,' but it's partly business. As I told you, I'm with Internal Revenue."

Into my throat again with my heart. "Internal Revenue. Oh, yes."

"You see, Mr. McNally, little Frankie has had so much fun playing with your children I thought I'd save you a little trouble. Since I live right down the street, I think the least I could do is to be a good neighbor."

I couldn't make out what he was driving at. All I could do was be polite, and ask him to keep talking. And he did.

"You see, since I work in the Bureau, a lot of forms and things pass over my desk. The other day the name and address on one looked familiar. I took a second look and knew it must be you. You're the only McNally on the street that I know of, so I thought I'd stop by on the way home from work and tip you off."

Tip me off to what?

"Well," he said, "this was one of the regular forms the

Bureau sends out. Apparently someone who has charge of your file sent you a letter asking you to come down and talk about a discrepancy in your tax return. And you apparently ignored the letter."

I opened my mouth to say something and thought better of it. Morton hurriedly went on.

"Now, Mr. McNally, I know you were gone most of the summer, and, since this is in my department, and since we're neighbors, I know that things get lost in the mail, and I thought I should drop by and tell you you must have never gotten any notice to appear. It might be a good idea for you to call in person, and explain what must have happened. It'd save you a lot of trouble, in the long run. Just tell them I stopped by on a friendly call."

He had more to say about that, but I think the situation really was that he didn't like the man who was in charge of my file, and wanted to warn me to get out from under before this someone really dropped the boom.

We talked for a little longer about his boy and mine and the things people talk about when they've met for the first time, and he left with an apologetic smile. He already felt he'd gone out of his way to mind someone else's business, and he felt guilty. I did my best to ease things, and Jean came out of the kitchen just before he left with a plate of cookies for Morton's wife.

We watched him go down the curving flagstone walk that had cost me two hundred duplicate dollars; we watched him walk briskly to his own house half a block away. I asked Jean if she wanted a cigarette. She shook her head.

"No. Not right now." She sat limply in the nearest chair. "Now what's going to happen to us?"

I told her I didn't know. But I'd take care of it.

She gave that short sarcastic laugh she saves for special occasions. "Yes, you'll take care of it. Like you take care of a lot of things. I knew you'd get in trouble sooner or later." I didn't know whether to get mad or to act sympathetic. When a woman cries, I don't think either one works. After I tossed a few words around I realized nothing was going to do much good, so I picked up my hat and went for a ride. I got into a card game at Art's, twenty miles away, where I hadn't been for some time. Art was so glad to see me he bought the house and me a beer, which, for Art, is exceptional. When I got home Jean was in bed pretending to be asleep. I let her keep up the pretense, and went to sleep myself.

The next morning, bright and early, with my heart in my mouth and lead in my shoes, I was standing in line at the counter in Federal Building. I told them what I was there for, and they passed me through three different hands and two different desks until I got to the man with my file.

The man had big ears and a bad disposition. His name was Johnson, and he made it quite clear that to me it was *Mr*. Johnson. He got right down to cases.

"You're lucky, McNally, that Frank Morton went out of his way to be neighborly, as he calls it. But that's neither here nor there. You haven't filed any income tax return for 1951, 1952, *and* for 1950. Why?"

I wasn't going to let him get me mad, but I knew I could make him blow his top. I detest public servants with an inferiority complex.

"Well, Johnson," I said, "for a good reason. For 1952, 1951, *and* 1950, I had no income."

That was just the answer he was looking for, and wasn't expecting. He shuffled papers like mad, unable to believe his luck.

"Well, now, McNally," he said triumphantly, "that's a rather peculiar statement. You have a house that is assessed at eight thousand dollars, and worth three times that. Right?"

Of course he was right. Taxes are low where I live, with the jet-engine plant paying most of the bills.

"And you have no income for three years, McNally, none at all?"

"Johnson," I told him sorrowfully. "I am a very law-abiding individual. I am quite familiar with the income tax rules" —which I wasn't—"and I am also a very thrifty person. My wife makes all my suits and raises all our food. I don't need income, but to overcome boredom I am thinking of applying for a government job, in the customer-relations department. Anything else, Mr. Johnson?"

No, there was nothing else. But "you'll quite possibly hear from us a little later, McNally." When I left he was frantically scribbling away with a red pencil. I certainly wish I didn't have such a lousy temper, but in for a lamb, in for a sheep. All I could do was to wait for the wheels to roll over me, with Johnson pressing the starting button.

The wheels rolled, and apparently missed me. We didn't hear from the Bureau of Internal Revenue all the rest of the year, and when next May came around Jean and I had almost forgotten. We decided it would be nice if we took a little trip, and found out that to go to Europe it would be necessary to get a passport. We applied for one. That must have been the trigger that made someone think we were trying to get out of Federal jurisdiction. We got no passports, but I got a summons.

It really wasn't a trial. There was no judge there, and I had no lawyer. We just sat down in uncomfortable chairs and faced each other. There isn't much use mentioning any names, so I won't. It was just a meeting to see if things could be settled without a trial; most likely because trials take up time and money. They were fairly decent, but it boiled down to this:

"Mr. McNally, you have a house, a car, and a bank account."

The bank account wasn't big, and I mentioned that.

"Big enough for someone with no income. And we can prove—actually *prove*—Mr. McNally, that in the past three years you have spent for tangibles almost twenty thousand dollars. Your scale of living is and has been running at a hundred dollars every week—or better."

I could do nothing but admit it, and compliment their thoroughness. They were not impressed.

"So, Mr. McNally, that is why you are here now. We see no use in subjecting you to the inconvenience of a trial, with all the attendant publicity."

They waited for me to agree with them, so I did.

"What we are primarily interested in, Mr. McNally, is not the exact amount of your income—although that is an extremely serious question, which must be adjusted to our satisfaction before this is all over."

That made me sit straight in the chair.

"Not so much in the amount, Mr. McNally, but the source. Just who are you working for, and how do you do it?"

Do what?

They were very patient, elaborately so. "How do you take the bets, Mr. McNally? How do they get the bets to you, and how do you pay off when you win or lose?"

"What bets?" I asked blankly. "What are you talking about?"

If you've never seen a collective lip being curled, you don't know what you've missed.

"Come now, Mr. McNally. Come now! We're all men of the world, if you want to put it that way. We know that you have a source of income. What we want to know—and we are *very* curious—is how you manage to run your business without using any means of communication we have been able to find."

They paused to let me consider; then: "We'll be frank with you, sir—we're puzzled. Puzzled so much that perhaps we can come to some sort of arrangement allowing you to pay your past-due taxes without penalty."

I began to laugh. First I laughed, and then I roared.

"I suppose," I said, "that you're the source of all the clicks and static we've been hearing on the telephone lately. And I imagine you're the source of all these cars and trucks that have been breaking down within a block of my house." They admitted it with their faces. "And you can't find out how I take bets, and how I pay off. And I'll bet that you're our new milkman, and our new baker!"

They let me laugh myself out, and they didn't like it. One of the government men stood up and towered over me.

"Mr. McNally, this is no laughing matter for you. You came here under your own power, and you may leave the same way if you so choose. But there is one thing I can definitely assure you; that you will be back here under less comfortable, more formal circumstances just as soon as we have presented the evidence we have against you to a Federal grand jury."

That didn't sound so good to me, and they all saw it.

"Did you, sir, ever stop to think what would happen to your wife and children if a true bill were presented against you? Are you prepared to face the penalty for deliberately neglecting to file an income tax return for three consecutive years? You cannot, regardless of how you are communicating with your runners, conduct a gambling business from a jail cell. Had you thought of that, Mr. McNally?"

The government men kept hammering at me and I kept thinking. A slim chance was better than no chance at all. Then they gave me my cue. Someone was saying: ". . . And you can't sit there and tell us you got all that income out of thin air!"

I broke in. "What did you say?"

"We were talking about the impossibility of your proving—"

"No. Go back a little. What you said about money out of thin air."

The collective smirk. "Let's not be too literal, Mr. McNally. We know you got the money; we want to know where and how you got it."

I told them. "Out of thin air, like you said." I slid out my billfold. "You might compare the numbers on these bills," and I passed out a handful. "The best place in the world to get money is right out of the air—no germs on it that way."

So they checked the serial numbers, and they compared the bills, and they began to scream like a herd of frustrated stallions. They were still screaming when I left, under my own power.

Probably the only reason they let me go was because I was so completely frank about everything.

"Never mind where I got the money," I said. "You admit you couldn't tell one from the other. If you'll come out to my house tomorrow I'll show you where they came from; keep me here and you'll be no further ahead than you are now."

One of them suggested they could follow other leads and nail me in the end—even if it took a couple years.

"But wouldn't you rather clean this up all in one shot? You know I wouldn't get far if I tried to skip, and I have no intention of doing that. Give me a chance to get things lined up—no, I have no one working with or for me, if that's what you're thinking—and tomorrow you get everything out in the open."

I didn't try to lose the car that followed me all the way home. Then I talked Jean into taking the kids over to her mother's the next morning, and drank three cans of beer before I could go to sleep.

The next morning I was shaved, dressed, and breakfasted when Jean and the kids pulled out of the driveway, bound for Grandma's. I knew that they would have a tail of some kind, but that was all to the good. When she was barely out on the main highway, away from the house, according to agreement, the Marines would land. They did—two quiet, insignificant-looking little men I had never seen before. But I've seen too many movies not to be able to spot a shoulder holster when I see one.

They were extremely polite, came in as though they were walking on expensive eggs. I gave them a pleasant smile and a can of beer apiece.

They introduced themselves as Internal Revenue and Secret Service, and I blinked at that. What was the Secret Service doing here? He told me.

"Secret Service is charged with the responsibility," he said, "of detecting and handling counterfeit money."

Well, I knew it had been a slim chance. All I could do was ride the horse, now that I'd ordered the saddle. I cleared my throat.

"Well, gentlemen, I asked you here deliberately. I think the best thing to do is to get this straightened out once and for all." Secret Service grunted. "And the best way to do it is make a clean breast of things. Right?"

"Right!"

I reached in my pocket. "Take a look at these. Are they counterfeit? Or are they good?" and I passed them a sheaf of bills.

Secret Service took them over to where the morning sun was glaring through the blinds and took a lens from his pocket. He stood there for quite some time before he came back to sit down.

I asked him, "Are they good, or are they bad?"

Secret Service grunted. "Perfectly good. Good as gold. Only they all have the same numbers."

"Fine," I said. "You probably don't get paid very much. Take them with you when you go." The temperature dropped forty degrees. I didn't have to be a mind reader to know why.

"No, I'm not trying to bribe you. I thought it would be a good illustration of what I said yesterday—that's right, you weren't there. Someone said that money doesn't come out of thin air. Well, this money did."

Internal Revenue believed that just as much as Secret Service, and said so.

I shrugged. "So you want a better sample?"

They nodded.

They had nothing to lose.

"How much money have you got on you? I don't mean silver, although I might be able to fix you up there, too, but bills. Dollar bills, fives, tens, twenties . . ." I tried to be funny. "Since you're not elected, I don't think you have any big bills." The joke fell flat, but between them they dug up about sixty dollars in bills of different denominations, and I spread them out as neatly as I could on the coffee table.

"All right, now; this is what I meant—" and I made sure that they were comfortably settled around the glass-topped surface. The first bill up in the right corner was a dollar, and I told them to watch the surface of the table right next to it. I looked at the bill and concentrated.

The surface of the glass clouded, and the duplicate began to appear, nice and green and shiny. When it was complete, I leaned back and told the pair to pick up the dollar and its mate and feel free to examine them. While they had the new one over under the light, looking at it from all angles, I did a quick job on the rest of the money and went out to the kitchen for more beer.

They were so intent on the first one they never saw me leave. When they turned back to me I was sitting there with a cigarette, three full cans, and an expectant smile. Then they looked at the coffee table and saw the rest of the duplicates.

Secret Service looked at the bills, at the ones he had in his hand, and at Internal Revenue. "Good God Almighty," he said, and collapsed into his chair.

It took some time for them to get their breath; longer still for them to be able to ask sensible questions.

"You probably won't believe me," I warned. "I still don't believe it myself."

Secret Service looked at Internal Revenue. "After that," he said, "I'll believe anything. Come on, McNally, you've got yourself into a mess. Let's hear you get yourself out of it."

That I couldn't go for. "I'm in no mess; you are. I'll make a million of those bills if you want, or if you don't, and all I can do is spend a few years in prison. Now, if I'm in trouble I'll stay in it. On the other hand, if you'll give me a clean bill of health I'll come across. Okay?"

Secret Service snorted. "My job is to nail the source of counterfeit money. Bud, you're all through!"

I kept after him. "Suppose you can say you've dried up the source. Suppose you can prove that to yourself, and your boss. Do I get a clean sheet? And do I get an okay for back taxes if I pay up?"

Internal Revenue hesitated. "Back taxes can always be paid up, with a penalty, if we think there was no criminal intent."

"And how about you?" I said to Secret Service. "Okay with you?"

But he was just as bullheaded as me. "No, McNally. You

stuck out your neck, and chopped it off yourself. You'll
make no more progress with U.S. currency."

I kept right after him. "All you can get me for is possession of what you call counterfeit money. It looks good to me.
Maybe the numbering machine stuck, or something."

"Yeah? No numbering machine in here. You made that
stuff right here in front of my eyes!"

"Did I?" I asked. "Maybe it was just a magic trick. The
hand is quicker than the eye, you know."

He was definite about that. "Not quicker than my eye.
You made that money right here in front of me. I don't know
how you did it, but I'll find out."

That was what I wanted him to say. "You saw me make
money right in front of you? Without a printing press or
anything? What would a jury say to that? What would they
think about your sanity—and yours?" I turned to Internal
Revenue. "And you still don't know how I did it, and you
never will, unless I tell you. Right? What do you say?"

Internal Revenue wagged his head and moaned. "Right,
I'm afraid."

Secret Service swore. "You too? You want to let this—
this counterfeiter get away with that? Why—"

I mentioned the old one about sticks and stones may
break my bones and he snorted hard enough to blow the
rest of the bills off the coffee table. No one picked them up.

"Well, how about it?" I prodded. "While you're thinking
about it, I'll get another beer."

"Oh no, you don't!" he yelped, and tried to follow me into
the kitchen. Internal Revenue pulled him back into his chair
and leaned over. I could hear them whispering frantically
while I pretended to have trouble finding the beer opener. I

let them whisper for two or three minutes until I went back into the living room and found the opener where it had been all the time. I opened the cans and sat back. Secret Service had a face like Thor.

"Make up your mind yet?" I inquired. "I'd like to coöperate, but not at the point of a gun."

His frown grew darker. "Got a telephone? I'll have to get my boss in on this."

Internal Revenue winced. "Yes, there's a phone. I've spent three months listening in on it." While Secret Service went to the phone to mutter briefly into it, I grinned. I know just how long Jean can talk to her mother saying absolutely nothing.

Secret Service came back and sat down. "He's pretty close to here. Five minutes."

We sat drinking cold beer until the boss showed up. Five minutes was a poor estimate. Three would have been better. I looked out the window and watched a telephone-company truck drop off an undistinguished repairman, and sit there with the motor running. Sharp babies, these Federals.

So we went through the whole routine again with the coffee table and the bills and I had the place littered with money before they all gave up. I began to wonder if there was enough beer.

The boss said, "What guarantee have I that this will stop?"

I said, "When you find out how I do it you'll be your own guarantee. Okay?"

The boss said, "No. There are a lot of things to be straightened out first. For one thing—"

I snapped at him, "Let's get this straight. I'll tell you how I make the money. I'll give you the gadget to take with you so you'll know I can't make any more. All you have to do is promise never to prosecute me for what's gone by in the past. Now, there's no strings to my offer—there'll be no more money made, and you let me alone for the rest of my life. If either of us ever breaks the agreement, everything is off and the other can do what he likes."

He jumped on one word. "Gadget! You make this stuff, really make it? It isn't just an optical illusion?"

I nodded. "I really make it, right in front of you, and if we do business you take the gadget with you right out the front door. Never again will I make a dime, and that's a promise!"

The boss looked at Secret Service and Secret Service looked at Internal Revenue. They all looked at me and I excused myself. When I came out of the bathroom they weren't too happy; the boss did the talking.

"McNally, God help you if you're lying. We'll coöperate, only because we have to. But, all right; we won't prosecute for anything you've done in the past. But, if you ever pull anything like this again, you're going to rue the day you were born. Just to show you I mean business, this could mean all our jobs. Counterfeiting is a felony, and we're letting you get away with it. Understand that?"

He barked out the words, and I knew he meant just what he said. But I meant what I'd said, too. I told him that was fair enough, as far as I was concerned.

"It'd better be. Now, start talking. How do you do it?"

I laughed. "I discovered it by accident. You can do it yourself. Here; this coffee table . . ."

They looked down at it. "What about it?"

"You're the boss," I told him. "You do it first. Just put

one of those bills on the glass and think about it. Think about how nice it would be if you had another one just like it. Think about where your next pay is going to go."

I'll give the boss credit. He hated to make a fool of himself, but he tried. He really tried. He took a bill out of his billfold and dropped it skeptically on the glass top. He shifted uncomfortably under the stares of the other two, and gave me one glare before he started concentrating on the money. Nothing happened.

He looked up at me and opened his mouth. I shook my head.

"This is no joke," I said softly. "You're the first one that knows this—even my wife doesn't," which was quite true.

He was game, and tried to concentrate. I motioned to Secret Service and Internal Revenue to move away with me, on the basis that the boss might find it a little easier without three men panting over him. We moved a few feet away and I took a sip of my beer.

I almost choked when I heard a gasp from the boss. I eagerly bent over the table again. The same thing was happening; the mist, the green color, the final completed bill. The boss sat up and wiped his forehead.

"Uh," he said.

"Let me try that," said Secret Service and Internal Revenue, almost in unison, and they in turn bent over the table. The same thing happened.

They all sat back and waited for me to talk. I sat back and waited for them to ask questions. The boss asked the first one.

"How do you do it?"

I told him the absolute truth. "I don't know. I was just sitting here with my wife one night, glooming about what we owed, when she took out the last ten dollars we had. She flipped it on the table to show me how short we were going to be, and I just sat there moping about life in general. The next thing you know we had two ten-dollar bills. And that was it."

They all moved back and looked at the coffee table.

The boss said, "Where did you get this—this portable mint?"

"From my relatives," I said. I went on to tell him about the banshees and the leprechauns and he didn't believe a word of it. But Secret Service did. Later I found out his name was Kelly.

"So what do we do now?" said the boss in an irritated voice.

"I told you that you could have the gadget," and I meant it. "I've got a home, a car, and enough money in the bank. I always thought I could write stories if I had the chance, and I've been waiting for a good one. I think this is it. Take the table, and good health with it."

He looked at the table again. "And anyone can work it—anyone at all?"

"I suppose so. You just did it yourself."

Without an instant's hesitation he smashed the muzzle of the gun down at the coffee table. There was an agonized tinkling crash that sounded feminine; and then there was nothing but brittle shards on the rug.

"Take this—thing outside," he commanded, and Secret Service carried the wooden frame of the table out on the front porch. The boss jumped on the skeleton until it shattered, and Secret Service himself brought a can of gasoline from the pseudo-telephone truck.

We all watched the wood burn until there were ashes that the wind carried away when I stirred them gently with my foot. Then they left together, without saying another word. I never saw any of them again; Kelly I recognized from his newspaper picture when he was promoted some years later.

So that's the story. I never made any duplicate bills again; my promise made, the table destroyed, the ashes lost in the breeze. I write a little on the side occasionally, and with my limited talent I don't sell too many stories. It's a good thing I had money in the bank when the table was burned; money isn't as easy to get as it once was.

Sometimes I regret losing the coffee table—it was an old family heirloom. And money was so easy to make when I had it, that life was a dream. But it's just as well that the boss smashed and burned it. If he had kept it for a while, he would have found out it was just a table, that *I* had made the bills while they were so intent on the money. It was my ancestry, and not theirs. But what they don't know will never hurt them. I kept my promise, and I'll go on keeping it. But I made no promises not to duplicate anything else.

Right now there's a lot of people engaged in the business of finding and restoring old automobiles. Next year I'm going to France to take a look at a Type 51 Bugatti. They cost forty thousand dollars to make twenty years ago, and there's only fourteen in existence. A fellow named Purdy who lives in New York would pay a good price for a fifteenth, I understand. And while I'm in Europe I'll just stop in and look at some rare books and stamps and coins. They tell me that's a good business, too—perfectly legal, and far more profitable than writing stories like this.

The last story, like the first, is about time. Fritz Leiber wrote this one in 1947 to fill out an Arkham House collection, *Night's Black Agents;* I think it is one of the most charming and hauntingly beautiful things he has ever done.

Fritz Leiber

THE MAN
WHO NEVER
GREW YOUNG

M aot is becoming restless. Often toward evening she
trudges to where the black earth meets the yellow sand and
stands looking across the desert until the wind starts.

But I sit with my back to the reed screen and watch the
Nile.

It isn't just that she's growing young. She is wearying of
the fields. She leaves their tilling to me and lavishes her at-
tentions on the flock. Every day she takes the sheep and
goats farther to pasture.

I have seen it coming for a long time. For generations the
fields have been growing scantier and less diligently irri-
gated. There seems to be more rain. The houses have
become simpler—mere walled tents. And every year some
family gathers its flocks and wanders off west.

Why should I cling so tenaciously to these poor relics of
civilization—I, who have seen king Cheops' men take down
the Great Pyramid block by block and return it to the hills?

I often wonder why I never grow young. It is still as
much a mystery to me as to the brown farmers who kneel in
awe when I walk past.

I envy those who grow young. I yearn for the sloughing
of wisdom and responsibility, the plunge into a period of
love-making and breathless excitement, the carefree years
before the end.

But I remain a bearded man of thirty-odd, wearing the goatskin as I once wore the doublet or the toga, always on the brink of that plunge yet never making it.

It seems to me that I have always been this way. Why, I cannot even remember my own disinterment, and everyone remembers that.

Maot is subtle. She does not ask for what she wants, but when she comes home at evening she sits far back from the fire and murmurs disturbing fragments of song and rubs her eyelids with green pigment to make herself desirable to me and tries in every way to infect me with her restlessness. She tempts me from the hot work at midday and points out how hardy our sheep and goats are becoming.

There are no young men among us any more. All of them start for the desert with the approach of youth, or before. Even toothless, scrawny patriarchs uncurl from their grave-holes, and hardly pausing to refresh themselves with the food and drink dug up with them, collect their flocks and wives and hobble off into the west.

I remember the first disinterment I witnessed. It was in a country of smoke and machines and constant news. But what I am about to relate occurred in a backwater where there were still small farms and narrow roads and simple ways.

There were two old women named Flora and Helen. It could not have been more than a few years since their own disinterments, but those I cannot remember. I think I was some sort of nephew, but I cannot be sure.

They began to visit an old grave in the cemetery a half mile outside town. I remember the little bouquets of flowers they would bring back with them. Their prim, placid faces became troubled. I could see that grief was entering their lives.

The years passed. Their visits to the cemetery became more frequent. Accompanying them once, I noted that the worn inscription on the headstone was growing clearer and sharper, just as was happening to their own features. "John, loving husband of Flora. . . ."

Often Flora would sob through half the night, and Helen went about with a set look on her face. Relatives came and spoke comforting words, but these seemed only to intensify their grief.

Finally the headstone grew brand-new and the grass became tender green shoots which disappeared into the raw brown earth. As if these were the signs their obscure instincts had been awaiting, Flora and Helen mastered their grief and visited the minister and the mortician and the doctor and made certain arrangements.

On a cold autumn day, when the brown curled leaves were whirling up into the trees, the procession set out—the empty hearse, the dark silent automobiles. At the cemetery we found a couple of men with shovels turning away unobtrusively from the newly opened grave. Then, while Flora and Helen wept bitterly, and the minister spoke solemn words, a long narrow box was lifted from the grave and carried to the hearse.

At home the lid of the box was unscrewed and slid back, and we saw John, a waxen old man with a long life before him.

Next day, in obedience to what seemed an age-old ritual, they took him from the box, and the mortician undressed him and drew a pungent liquid from his veins and injected the red blood. Then they took him and laid him in bed. After a few hours of stony-eyed waiting, the blood began to work. He stirred and his first breath rattled in his throat. Flora sat down on the bed and strained him to her in a fearful embrace.

But he was very sick and in need of rest, so the doctor waved her from the room. I remember the look on her face as she closed the door.

I should have been happy too, but I seem to recall that I felt there was something unwholesome about the whole episode. Perhaps our first experiences of the great crises of life always affect us in some such fashion.

I love Maot. The hundreds I have loved before her in my wanderings down the world do not take away from the sincerity of my affection. I did not enter her life, or theirs, as lovers ordinarily do—from the grave or in the passion of some terrible quarrel. I am always the drifter.

Maot knows there is something strange about me. But she does not let that interfere with her efforts to make me do the thing she wants.

I love Maot and eventually I will accede to her desire. But first I will linger awhile by the Nile and the mighty pageantry conjured up by its passage.

My first memories are always the most difficult and I struggle the hardest to interpret them. I have the feeling that if I could get back a little beyond them, a terrifying understanding would come to me. But I never seem able to make the necessary effort.

They begin without antecedent in cloud and turmoil, darkness and fear. I am a citizen of a great country far away, beardless and wearing ugly confining clothing, but no different in age and appearance from today. The country is a hundred times bigger than Egypt, yet it is only one of many. All the peoples of the world are known to each other, and the world is round, not flat, and it floats in an endless immensity dotted with islands of suns, not confined under a star-speckled bowl.

Machines are everywhere, and news goes round the world like a shout, and desires are many. There is undreamed-of abundance, unrivaled opportunities. Yet men are not happy. They live in fear. The fear, if I recall rightly, is of a war that will engulf and perhaps destroy some enemy city. Others that dart up beyond the air itself, to come in attacking from the stars. Poisoned clouds. Deadly motes of luminous dust.

But worst of all are the weapons that are only rumored.

For months that seem eternities we wait on the brink of that war. We know that the mistakes have been made, the irrevocable steps taken, the last chances lost. We only await the event.

It would seem that there must have been some special reason for the extremity of our hopelessness and horror. As if there had been previous worldwide wars and we had struggled back from each desperately promising ourselves that it would be the last. But of any such, I can remember nothing. I and the world might well have been created under the shadow of that catastrophe, in a universal disinterment.

The months wear on. Then, miraculously, unbelievably, the war begins to recede. The tension relaxes. The clouds lift. There is great activity, conferences and plans. Hopes for lasting peace ride high.

This does not last. In sudden holocaust, there arises an

oppressor named Hitler. Odd, how that name should come back to me after these millennia. His armies fan out across the globe.

But their success is short-lived. They are driven back, and Hitler trails off into oblivion. In the end he is an obscure agitator, almost forgotten.

Another peace then, but neither does it last. Another war, less fierce than the preceding, and it too trails off into a quieter era.

And so on.

I sometimes think (I must hold on to this) that time once flowed in the opposite direction, and that, in revulsion from the ultimate war, it turned back upon itself and began to retrace its former course. That our present lives are only a return and an unwinding. A great retreat.

In that case time may turn again. We may have another chance to scale the barrier.

But no . . .

The thought has vanished in the rippling Nile.

Another family is leaving the valley today. All morning they have toiled up the sandy gorge. And now, returning perhaps for a last glimpse, to the verge of the yellow cliffs, they are outlined against the morning sky—upright specks for men, flat specks for animals.

Maot watches beside me. But she makes no comment. She is sure of me.

The cliff is bare again. Soon they will have forgotten the Nile and its disturbing ghosts of memories.

All our life is a forgetting and a closing in. As the child is absorbed by its mother, so great thoughts are swallowed up in the mind of genius. At first they are everywhere. They environ us like the air. Then there is a narrowing in. Not all men know them. Then there comes one great man, and he takes them to himself, and they are a secret. There only remains the disturbing conviction that something worthy has vanished.

I have seen Shakespeare unwrite the great plays. I have watched Socrates unthink the great thoughts. I have heard Jesus unsay the great words.

There is an inscription in stone, and it seems eternal. Coming back centuries later I find it the same, only a little less worn, and I think that it, at least, may endure. But some day a scribe comes and laboriously fills in the grooves until there is only blank stone.

Then only he knows what was written there. And as he grows young, that knowledge dies forever.

It is the same in all we do. Our houses grow new and we dismantle them and stow the materials inconspicuously away, in mine and quarry, forest and field. Our clothes grow new and we put them off. And we grow new and forget and blindly seek a mother.

All the people are gone now. Only I and Maot linger.

I had not realized it would come so soon. Now that we are near the end, Nature seems to hurry.

I suppose that there are other stragglers here and there along the Nile, but I like to think that we are the last to see the vanishing fields, the last to look upon the river with some knowledge of what it once symbolized, before oblivion closes in.

Ours is a world in which lost causes conquer. After the second war of which I spoke, there was a long period of peace in my native country across the sea. There were among us at that time a primitive people called Indians, neglected and imposed upon and forced to live apart in unwanted areas. We gave no thought to these people. We would have laughed at anyone who told us they had power to hurt us.

But from somewhere a spark of rebellion appeared among them. They formed bands, armed themselves with bows and inferior guns, took the warpath against us.

We fought them in little unimportant wars that were never quite conclusive. They persisted, always returning to the fight, laying ambushes for our men and wagons, harrying us continually, eventually making sizable inroads.

Yet we still considered them of such trifling importance that we found time to engage in a civil war among ourselves.

The issue of this war was sad. A dusky portion of our citizenry were enslaved and made to toil for us in house and field.

The Indians grew formidable. Step by step they drove us back across the wide midwestern rivers and plains, through the wooded mountains to eastward.

On the eastern coast we held for a while, chiefly by leaguing with a transoceanic island nation, to whom we surrendered our independence.

There was an enheartening occurrence. The enslaved Negroes were gathered together and crowded in ships and taken to the southern shores of this continent, and there liberated or given into the hands of warlike tribes who eventually released them.

But the pressure of the Indians, sporadically aided by foreign allies, increased. City by city, town by town, settlement by settlement, we pulled up our stakes and took ship ourselves across the sea. Toward the end the Indians became strangely pacific, so that the last boatloads seemed to flee not so much in physical fear as in supernatural terror of the green silent forests that had swallowed up their homes.

To the south the Aztecs took up their glass knives and flint-edged swords and drove out the . . . I think they were called Spaniards.

In another century the whole western continent was forgotten, save for dim, haunting recollections.

Growing tyranny and ignorance, a constant contraction of frontiers, rebellions of the downtrodden, who in turn became oppressors—these constituted the next epoch of history.

Once I thought the tide had turned. A strong and orderly people, the Romans, arose and put most of the diminished world under their sway.

But this stability proved transitory. Once again the governed rose against the governors. The Romans were driven back—from England, from Egypt, from Gaul, from Asia, from Greece. Rising from barren fields came Carthage to contest successfully Rome's preëminence. The Romans took refuge in Rome, became unimportant, dwindled, were lost in a maze of migrations.

Their energizing thoughts flamed up for one glorious century in Athens, then ceased to carry weight.

After that, the decline continued at a steady pace. Never again was I deceived into thinking the trend had changed.

Except this one last time.

Because she was stony and sun-drenched and dry, full of temples and tombs, given to custom and calm, I thought

Egypt would endure. The passage of almost changeless centuries encouraged me in this belief. I thought that if we had not reached the turning point, we had at least come to rest.

But the rains have come, the temples and tombs fill the scars in the cliffs, and the custom and calm have given way to the restless urges of the nomad.

If there is a turning point, it will not come until man is one with the beasts.

And Egypt must vanish like the rest.

Tomorrow Maot and I set out. Our flock is gathered. Our tent is rolled.

Maot is afire with youth. She is very loving.

It will be strange in the desert. All too soon we will exchange our last and sweetest kiss and she will prattle to me childishly and I will look after her until we find her mother.

Or perhaps some day I will abandon her in the desert, and her mother will find her.

And I will go on.